Can't resist a sexy military hero?

Then you'll love our **Uniformly Hot!** miniseries.

Harlequin Blaze's bestselling miniseries
continues with more irresistible soldiers
from all branches of the armed forces.

Don't miss

A SEAL'S KISS

by Tawny Weber

April 2014

WICKED SEXY

by Anne Marsh

July 2014

COMMAND CONTROL

by Sara Jane Stone

August 2014

Blaze®

Dear Reader,

From the moment I started writing Jace and Quinn's story I knew it was going to be one of those that grabbed my heart and refused to let go. They're both dealing with such deep, sometimes heart-wrenching issues. And if their personal demons weren't enough, I had to throw in another character finally finding the strength to leave a situation involving domestic violence. But I hope all their struggles only make you root for them to find happiness even more—I know that's what happened for me.

Jace and Quinn have struggled for years against wanting each other and feeling as if they're betraying the memory of someone they both love. The great thing about love is that it's fathomless. Loving one person doesn't mean you can't love someone else just as much, although maybe a little differently. The heart has such a limitless capacity for compassion.

I hope that's the message everyone takes away from Testing the Limits—not just because Jace and Quinn finally find a way to accept what they share, but because of the way they both selflessly give of themselves to help others. In this respect, they are amazingly similar and make me want to be a better person.

I'd love to hear from you at www.kirasinclair.com, or come chat with me on Twitter: @KiraSinclair.

Best wishes,

Kira

Kira Sinclair

—

Testing the Limits

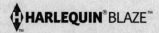
HARLEQUIN® BLAZE™

Recycling programs for this product may not exist in your area.

ISBN-13: 978-0-373-79804-9

TESTING THE LIMITS

Copyright © 2014 by Kira Bazzel

Printed in U.S.A.

www.Harlequin.com

ABOUT THE AUTHOR

Kira Sinclair is an award-winning author who writes emotional, passionate contemporary romances. Double winner of the National Readers' Choice Award, her first foray into writing fiction was for a high-school English assignment. Nothing could dampen her enthusiasm...not even being forced to read the love story aloud to the class. However, it definitely made her blush. Writing about striking, sexy heroes and passionate, determined women has always excited her. She lives out her own happily-ever-after with her amazing husband, their two beautiful daughters and a menagerie of animals on a small farm in North Alabama. Kira loves to hear from readers at www.kirasinclair.com.

Books by Kira Sinclair

HARLEQUIN BLAZE

*Island Nights

To get the inside scoop on Harlequin Blaze and its talented writers, be sure to check out blazeauthors.com.

All backlist available in ebook format.

I'd like to dedicate this book to anyone who has registered to become an organ and tissue donor. It's such an important and selfless gift, and your sacrifice can help save someone else's life. However, it isn't enough to sign your driver's license or register online. You have to tell the people closest to you what your wishes are—share your intent to give the gift of life.

For more information on organ donation please visit www.organdonor.gov.

1

QUINN KELLER DIDN'T often lose it. She tried hard to keep a rein on her temper. It was something she'd been working on her entire life, not wanting to hurt others with harsh words. Most days she succeeded.

She gritted her teeth, her body quivering with barely suppressed fury. Today wasn't one of those days.

Luckily, the object of her rage deserved every last speck of it, and she wouldn't lose one wink of sleep over anything she said.

Slick and condescending, Everett Warren thought he was above the rules. It had taken everything she had not to slam her fist into his smug face. Fortunately, her brain was working faster than her instincts for once, because if she'd given in to the urge she probably would have lost her job.

And then how would she be able to help Caroline Warren, the asshole's wife?

"There's been a grave misunderstanding, Ms. Keller," Warren had said, in that deep, solemn voice that was probably supposed to indicate just how important and trustworthy a man he was.

Unfortunately for him, Quinn had seen the evidence of the opposite with her own eyes.

An image of Caroline's body, marked and bruised, flashed across Quinn's mind. Not twelve hours ago she'd held the woman's hand while a doctor and nurse had taken care of her injuries. She'd been there as Caroline had stripped naked so they could take pictures of the damage for evidence. And the marks hadn't all been from last night. Several of the bruises were days and weeks old. All purposely positioned so they could be well covered.

And then Quinn had hidden Caroline in a safe house on a small farm on the outskirts of town.

Somehow, despite Warren's false concern, Quinn managed to bite her tongue, keeping the snide comments to herself. Misunderstanding, her ass. She hated men who felt putting a ring on a woman's finger equaled the right to dictate, intimidate and hit.

What made Warren worse than most was the smooth exterior he presented to the world. Most of the abusers she'd met over the years didn't bother pretending they were anything else. They didn't care enough to hide the truth.

Warren did. In fact, he worked hard at the perfect facade. He was a major donor to several high-profile charities in town. He'd won service awards and been hailed as a town hero for years. Hell, even she'd been sucked in by the pretense. How could she not be? He'd funded several of the programs for the people she assisted on a daily basis.

Although, according to Caroline, the money he'd been liberally spreading around town for years wasn't exactly clean. Certainly, he had legitimate business interests. But also ties with "families" that were well known for their ruthless behavior.

To put it bluntly, he laundered money.

The minute Caroline had told her that, Quinn had tried to call in the cops. But Caroline had flipped at the idea of talking to them. She was scared—not just of Warren, but also the men he worked for. Considering the evidence Quinn had seen, Caroline had good reason for that fear.

So Quinn had planned on giving Caroline a few days to settle in and begin to feel safe before pressing the issue again.

They had to proceed with caution, anyway.

Warren had money, a sense of entitlement and played poker at least once a month with a judge, several lawyers, two city councilmen and most of the financial heavy hitters in Barnhart, their small town just outside Fort Benning, Georgia. He'd built a network of friends and associates who'd back him first and ask questions later.

And Quinn didn't want Caroline to be their target.

She'd known Warren would be pissed. What she hadn't expected was a personal visit from the man.

"At least let me speak to her. I need to know she's okay."

His words held so much sincerity and concern Quinn almost wanted to believe him. And maybe she would have, if she hadn't seen the truth lurking deep beneath the surface.

He'd smiled at her pleasantly, even as his eyes had glinted hard and promised retribution. A silent shiver of apprehension shot down Quinn's spine.

Working as a counselor for a nonprofit assistance

center that handled everything from court ordered drug programs and referrals from local shelters, to those who came in off the street looking for help, she'd seen some pretty shitty stuff. It shouldn't amaze her just how unfeeling the human race could be. Unfortunately, the moment she thought she'd seen the worst, someone like Warren came along and proved her wrong.

The problem was that Warren was too damn smart. He knew just what he could and couldn't say.

He hadn't actually threatened her *or* Caroline. He'd intimated that he was willing to pull all his financial support from their programs. When that hadn't gotten him anywhere, he'd started playing hardball, smoothly suggesting he not only knew exactly where Quinn lived, but could, with little effort, discover things like the name of her third-grade teacher, her credit score and where she liked to buy her gourmet coffee.

Not enough to qualify as an actual threat, but more than enough to give her the heebie-jeebies. And make Daniel, her boss, worry.

Which only pissed her off more. And may have driven her to throw a coffee mug in the break room after Warren left. Something she wasn't particularly proud of but…the coward couldn't even threaten her properly. He hadn't given her enough to file an incident report with the police.

But Quinn refused to let the prick intimidate her.

Unlike his wife, Quinn wasn't afraid of Warren. His words couldn't hurt her. It was one thing to beat a woman he had easy access to and thought he could control. Quinn was another matter. It would take effort to get to her and she seriously didn't think he'd bother. By not giving in to his intimidation she'd proven threatening her wouldn't work. So now he'd most likely try to find another—easier—way to get what he wanted.

Bullies were usually lazy.

Daniel, however, wasn't so quick to dismiss him. "I want you to head home. You had a long night and deserve some downtime."

Quinn saw right through the ruse. But even as it irked her, she couldn't stop herself from appreciating the sentiment behind the gesture.

"Not necessary," she'd protested.

Daniel frowned, a tight line pulling between his bushy black eyebrows. "I insist, Quinn. Will you just, for once, not argue?"

She scoffed, a harsh sound scraping through her throat. "We both know how likely that is."

"Don't make me revoke your access to the server."

She sucked in a hard breath. "You wouldn't do that."

"Don't bet on it." Walking around her desk, he planted his wide hips on the edge and leaned down toward her. The skin at the edges of his eyes pulled tight, doubling the wrinkles that already radiated out into his receding hairline. "Quinn, you need a break. We all need a break. Last night was intense. Warren's visit only made it worse."

"But I have a ton of cases that need my attention." Both of their gazes scraped across the top of Quinn's desk. It was messy, littered with files piled haphazardly on top of one another. Papers stuck out of several of them. Post-it Notes in all the shades of the rainbow clung to every available surface.

It was ordered chaos, just the way she liked it.

But she didn't miss Daniel's wince when he took it all in.

She'd lost the argument.

Unfortunately, not only would her cases still be there waiting in the morning, no doubt more would have been piled on. There were days she wondered why she put herself through the wringer. Kids being beaten and starved. Addicts spiraling out of control, unwilling to accept help. Runaways. Veterans feeling lost and broken. Women being treated like property. Hungry, desperate and emotionally devastated people—that's what she dealt with all day.

The ones who fell through the cracks or didn't think they deserved better broke her heart the most. Some days she left the office with a seemingly permanent ache in the center of her chest.

It was hard, seeing that kind of devastation and desperation. It wore on a person. But just when she'd get to the point where she thought she couldn't take one more, something would always happen to remind her why she could. A runaway was reunited with a parent. A drug addict went into treatment. Or a battered woman discovered the strength to leave.

Those were the days she felt she was making a difference in people's lives. Just as others had made a difference in her life when she'd needed it most.

So Warren could try his best, but there was no way in hell Quinn was giving him a damn thing. It had taken courage for Caroline to leave, and Quinn wasn't repaying that by abandoning her.

Pulling up to the house she'd purchased over two years ago, Quinn sat in her car and stared at the sunny yellow siding.

A memory, one she hadn't thought about in a very long time, swelled up to overwhelm her. The moment Michael had seen the place he'd known it was home. She hadn't been as convinced.

Pulling her out of the car, he'd coaxed her down the cracked walk. "Come on, baby, you're gonna love it. Promise."

He'd tried to butter her up, wrapping his arms around her waist and nibbling on her neck as they'd closed in on the front door.

It had almost worked, although not even his enthusiasm could mask the flaws. "The walk is all cracked. And the paint's peeling off the door."

"Easily fixed. That's cosmetic stuff. What you can't change is the history of the house or the fantastic school district."

"School district?" She couldn't hide the squeak of surprise. Swallowing, she'd tried to force down the knot of anxiety and dread that had threatened to choke her. After three years of dating, she'd just finally agreed to marry him. And he'd instantly had them pushing strollers and walking toddlers to kindergarten.

Always tuned into her reactions, Michael had smoothed his hands down her bare arms and turned her softly to face him. "Not now. I know we're not ready. But some day, yeah?"

God, what she wouldn't give to go back to that day and let him get her pregnant right then and there. That way she'd still have a piece of him, one she could kiss and hug and love.

As always, Michael had been able to talk his way into what he wanted. Although, by the time they were finished with the grand tour Quinn hadn't minded. She'd fallen in love with the house as surely as he had.

They'd bought it together. Michael, ever planning for the future, had insisted on the insurance that would pay off the mortgage should anything happen to either of them. She'd scoffed. Michael was a finance guy, far from living life on the edge. They were both young.

Little did they know that five months later Michael would be gone. It had happened so fast....

With a sigh, Quinn pushed away the sad thoughts. Not for the first time, she wondered if maybe she should sell the place. It had been two years. And the house was big. Too big for one person.

Unlocking the front door, she pushed inside the cool foyer. Dropping her purse onto the antique bench she kept by the entrance, she toed off her ballet flats and nudged them beneath it.

No, she didn't want to give up the place. It had been hers longer than hers and Michael's. It was home.

Padding to the back of the house and her bedroom, she was already fantasizing about ditching her bra, putting on yoga pants and curling up with a good book.

But passing by the wide picture window in her den, she froze.

It wasn't every day she came home to a sweaty man mowing her back lawn. Especially a man with his shirt off, muscles rippling down his back with every shove of her ancient push mower over the grass.

For a few minutes, she had the luxury of watching him work. Or maybe she was just dumbstruck and unable to move. Her body flushed hot, as if the air conditioning had stopped working and the hot June air had rushed in.

Running her tongue across suddenly parched lips, she couldn't tear her gaze away from him. Or the twisting gray, black and red ink down his right arm, a helicopter surrounded by flames and chaos behind a group of shadowy soldiers, two holding one up. That was Jace

Hyland to a T, always holding up the people around him, sacrificing and supporting with a silent austerity that mostly intimidated.

Every time she saw it, that tattoo made the center of her chest hurt. It was an amazing piece of art, but it was the emotion behind it that got to her. That, and the silent reminder that Jace was the kind of man who put himself in harm's way without hesitation.

However, it was the huge angel wings, feathers so detailed Quinn thought they might lift straight off his body and take flight, spread wide across his broad shoulders that always made her throat tighten and close. They were for Michael.

As was the swirl of black ink, a scrolling tribal pattern that snaked up from the band of Jace's loose gym shorts over his abs, left hip and up his ribs, camouflaging the scars.

Not that either of them would ever forget they existed. Four of them. The biggest one was just below and to the left of his belly button where they'd taken out his kidney. Another smaller one above and two more along his side where the cameras had been inserted.

The only reason she knew they were there was because she'd seen them before the stark black marks had covered up the pink, puckered flesh.

The familiar knot dropped into Quinn's stomach, dread, grief and something she'd been fighting for a very long time—interest.

She thought about leaving, just walking back out the door and pretending she hadn't seen him. But before she could move, he reached the end of the row he was mowing, turned and, with the instincts she knew he'd honed over years in hostile territory, zeroed right in on her standing there gawking.

He held her gaze for several moments, too far away for Quinn to really decipher his expression. Then he left the mower and crossed her lawn in sure, powerful strides that ate up ground and left her insides a little shaky.

The sound of the door bouncing against her kitchen wall echoed deep inside her chest, rumbling and rattling and skittering across her skin with a flush of something she really didn't want to think about. Didn't want to want.

It had been weeks since they'd seen each other. Jace made a point of checking in with her—usually by arranging to meet for dinner—at least once a month. Those nights were often strained and fraught with things neither of them wanted to say, so Quinn ate quickly and disappeared as fast as possible.

She knew Jace viewed those nights as an obligation. A promise he'd made to his dying brother. Quinn hated feeling like a burden—especially when being around the man made her feel things she wasn't ready to acknowledge. But the few times she'd told Jace his obligation had been fulfilled, the man had simply stared at her with those crystal-clear eyes, his mouth hard and his jaw set in a way that told her the subject wasn't up for debate.

So she'd stopped trying to get out of the dinners, instead concentrating on just getting through them. They never talked about Michael or his work. In fact, Jace rarely spoke about anything, but he definitely had no issues interrogating her about her life.

It was a good thing she usually had plenty of stories

about cases, otherwise they'd eat in silence. And that wouldn't help her nerves at all.

But none of that explained what he was doing at her house in the middle of the day.

Well, yeah, it was obvious *what* he was doing— mowing her lawn. Someone had been doing it for quite a while. And plenty of other things, too, like cutting back her bushes, taking her trash to the street, fixing the squeaky back door, and replacing broken screens and shingles. She'd assumed it was one of her neighbors, although all of them had denied it when she'd asked.

Apparently, they weren't lying to save her ego.

Jace rounded the corner, pulling a T-shirt over his head to hide those gorgeous abs. Her mouth opened to protest, although her brain was quick enough to cut off the words before they broke free. Instead she asked, "What are you doing here?"

He stopped in the doorway, arms stretching above his head to grip the lintel. Even from several feet away, Quinn could see the fading bruises bleeding across the edge of his hard jaw.

Shaking her head, she took a single step forward, her hand already reaching for him. She needed to get a better look to determine if there was anything she could do for him.

With a quick jerk of his head he stopped her. "You don't want to do that. I'm all hot and sweaty. I probably smell like a locker room."

Quinn frowned. "I'm sure I've experienced worse." Stepping close, she placed a soft finger beneath his chin and urged him to turn and let her see. He resisted, the muscles in his neck tightening before finally letting go. With a sigh, he turned.

The pad of her finger scraped down his cheek, energy and a day's worth of stubble crackling across her skin. "Do I want to know?"

He chuckled, the sound barely more than a soft gust of air. "Probably not."

Frustration and something more dangerous flooded her. "Jesus, Jace, when are you going to stop punishing yourself? What happened to Michael was not your fault."

His body stiffened. Every already-hard muscle went even more rock solid. Quinn placed her hands on his shoulders, hoping the contact might ease his pain.

He'd been there for her. Helped her through those first few months when she was close to useless with grief. He'd brought her food. Called in friends. Silently watched over her because she'd been incapable of doing that for herself.

And she'd leaned on him, using everything he gave her without thought or question. Now she regretted those months more than anything she'd ever done.

Blinded by her own grief, she'd missed the signs that Jace was struggling just as surely as she was… maybe more.

Foolishly, he blamed himself for his brother's death. In reality, he'd been the one trying to save him, selflessly giving Michael a kidney when he'd come back as a match. Jace hadn't hesitated—no one had expected him to. He did have a bit of a hero complex. But the sacrifice had cost him. With only one kidney, he'd had to give up something he lived for—being deployed with the Rangers.

Oh, he was still in the military, now stationed with the Ranger Training Brigade, but everyone knew it wasn't the same thing. Jace got off on the danger and adrenaline, but with little more than thirty seconds of contemplation he'd given it all up.

When Michael developed complications after the surgery, for some reason Jace felt he'd failed his brother. Failed her.

And no matter how often she told him he was wrong, he just wouldn't let the guilt go.

Slowly, he turned to look at her, his blue eyes blazing. "I know it wasn't my fault."

Pain and sorrow tightened her chest. Running the pad of her thumb over his skin she whispered, "I don't think you do."

Jerking away from her, he fell back into the kitchen, turning away under the guise of grabbing some water.

She'd tried to have this conversation with him enough times to realize she wasn't getting anywhere. He'd shut down and shut her out. Just as he'd been doing with everyone for the past two years.

Fine. "What are you doing here?" she asked again.

In a tone that implied the question had been silly the first time and downright ignorant the second, he said, "Mowing your lawn."

"Thanks, smartass. I meant *why*. While I was at work. Without telling me."

"Because I know you, Quinn. If I'd asked, you'd have come up with some excuse for me not to."

"That's because I'm perfectly capable of handling it myself."

"Sure, but you don't have to. Michael asked me to look out for you and that's what I'm doing."

"Somehow I don't think he meant by mowing my lawn and replacing shingles."

Jace tagged her with a calculating glance from beneath long, inky lashes, no doubt trying to assess just how much she knew—or had figured out.

Her mouth twisted into a grimace. The answer was enough. "Michael's gone and has been for a while. I'm fine. You don't have to keep watching over me."

He couldn't hide his wince, and she immediately regretted her words. That brief flash of pain across his face made her want to cringe. It was getting harder and harder to be around him. Not because he reminded her of Michael…because he didn't.

When she looked at Jace Hyland the *last* thing on her mind was the man she'd lost. Which just made her feel guilty and…overheated. Especially considering Jace had never given her the slightest indication he thought of her as anything except his almost sister-in-law.

Frustration fizzing uncomfortably beneath her skin, she whispered, "I'm sorry. I didn't mean that the way it sounded."

Closing the gap between them, Quinn laid her hand on his arm. A zap of electricity sparked through her fingers, but she ignored it.

"Look, I appreciate what you're trying to do, but it isn't necessary."

In true Jace fashion, he completely ignored what she said. "What are you doing home early?"

2

GOD, HE WANTED to touch her. Pull her into his arms and just bury his face in the soft cloud of brown-blond hair. The scent of her, something so sweet and tempting, filled his lungs.

He'd spent the past two years trying to keep some space between them, honor Michael's memory and control his damn body whenever Quinn got close.

It killed him, trying to pretend he didn't want his brother's fiancée and had since long before Michael died.

That realization just added to the pile of guilt he already carried around with him, a permanent weight settled across his shoulders.

He tried to tell himself it was nothing more than a physical response. What man wouldn't want Quinn Keller? She was gorgeous in an effortless, understated way. She was real, not bothering with the pretense that other women in their late twenties seemed to need—lots of make-up, flashy clothes, jewelry and heels.

She didn't waste her time at expensive salons. Why would she when her chestnut hair had natural blond highlights, the kind women spent a fortune to get? Most of the time she kept it up in a bun or a ponytail, but he'd seen it down a few times over the years. And those memories…those were the ones that starred in his midnight fantasies.

Hair tangled in a mess down her naked back. His hands buried deep in the thick strands, holding her still as he claimed her mouth and made them both breathless.

The intriguing caramel color of her eyes. The way they flashed with flecks of gold when she was angry, impassioned…or heartbroken.

But it was her skin that really tormented him. So pale. So soft. And covered with freckles that gave her the illusion of being younger than she actually was.

If it weren't for her large, pouty mouth she'd probably come off innocent as a nun. That mouth…

Jace stared down at her, unable to do anything but watch as her lips moved. The familiar burn seared across his skin. It settled into his gut, caustic and poisonous.

He couldn't have her. He couldn't touch her.

She was not his.

But, God, he wanted her.

When she was this close, it was so damn hard to remember why he needed to keep his distance.

He leaned closer. The warmth of her body slipped out to touch him, as surely as any caress. He was cold. Had been for a very long time. And while he knew the torture that awaited him when this moment was over, he couldn't stop himself from taking and absorbing whatever he could for now.

The numbing pain and guilt would be back soon enough.

The relief Quinn always gave him was bittersweet. Amazing while he had it. But the crash back into darkness seemed to get exponentially more painful with each encounter.

"Jace, are you listening?"

Her soft voice cut through the fog. Jace curled his hands into fists and forced himself to think about something else. The MMA fight that was coming up tomorrow night. The one he'd been training months for.

He flexed his fingers before curling them tight again. Imagined his knuckles split and bleeding. The relief of a pain he could see, feel, understand and combat...unlike the constant ache he'd been unsuccessfully battling for the past two years.

Taking a step backward, Jace put distance between them. Quinn frowned, her eyes flashing with disappointment and hurt, but there wasn't anything he could do about that. He could either do this or something they'd both regret.

Quinn was the last connection he had to Michael, outside of his family, and as much as being around her was personal torture, he couldn't give that up.

He couldn't give her up.

"I'm sorry, Quinn. It's been a long day."

He'd taken a couple weeks' leave, not because he particularly cared about time off, but so he could prepare for this fight...and recover when it was over. He'd been at the gym at four this morning and spent ten hours punishing his body in preparation.

He needed these nights, for his sanity. Even if his doctors had warned him about the dangers of participating in such a high-contact sport.

He missed the physical tests and mental challenges

of combat. The thrill and adrenaline high he got from pushing his body and mind past their limits. Since he couldn't go into combat anymore, he'd found a substitute—amateur mixed martial arts.

No one in his life was particularly happy that he was doing it—especially his mother. But he craved this outlet. So most of the time he didn't bother telling anyone about a fight until it was already done.

What his mom didn't know about, she didn't have to obsessively worry over.

Quinn tried to close the gap between them, compassion and concern clouding her beautiful eyes. Jace countered her move by taking another step back.

Her mouth flattened, and a deep sigh slipped through her lush lips.

"Never mind." She turned away, heading down the hall.

A band tightened across his chest. Before he could stop and think he shot after her. Hand wrapped around her arm, he steered her back around to face him.

"Tell me."

She shook her head. His grip on her arm tightened.

"Fine. Daniel sent me home because the husband of a woman I placed in a safe house last night came by the office and made some threats."

Jace growled low in the back of his throat. The sound was out before he contemplated making it.

"What kind of threats?"

Placing her hand on his, Quinn gently pried his fingers loose. Jace glanced down and saw the faint pink marks he'd left on her pale skin. He tried to jerk his hand away, but she refused to let go.

"Nothing concrete. He threatened to pull funding for some of our programs."

"Does he have that kind of influence?"

She frowned, a tiny pucker pulling at the space between her eyes. "Unfortunately."

"But why would Daniel send you home over something like that?"

Quinn's gaze dropped to the floor between them. Heat slowly crept up her skin. She directed her words down, as if she could bury them there. "I may have lost my temper and thrown a coffee mug."

He made a choked sound, biting back a response that was equal parts shock, exasperation and laughter.

Only Quinn.

"Please tell me it wasn't aimed at his head."

"Nope, he was already gone."

Thank God for small favors. Jace didn't want to think what the guy's reaction might have been if she'd hit a man who was clearly comfortable with beating his own wife.

"So he didn't send you home because he was worried?"

"No, Daniel was plenty worried. Everett Warren is ruthless and cold."

"Everett Warren?" Jace asked, his voice grim. Everyone in town knew the man, although not everyone realized just how crooked he really was.

The only reason Jace knew was because some of the guys he trained with worked for Warren, and not in his fancy office building.

While he didn't have details, he knew enough to be wary.

And now Quinn was on the guy's radar. Not just that, but she was standing between him and his wife.

An uncomfortable knot tightened in his belly.

"I don't like this, Quinn."

"Yeah, I'm not exactly thrilled with it myself. Caroline's told me enough, but until I can convince her to talk to the police there's not much I can do. Except make sure he can't get to her."

That wasn't what he meant.

"You need to be careful. Warren isn't the kind of man you mess with."

"I'm not afraid of him."

"Maybe you should be. He obviously hurt his wife so he's more than capable of hurting you."

Quinn shrugged, dismissing the threat as if it didn't even exist. That only made Jace's teeth clench harder. God, she was stubborn.

"Caroline was a convenient target. I'm not."

Apparently, they had different definitions for convenient. It wasn't as if Quinn was hiding. She'd be easy enough to find, especially for someone with Warren's network of connections.

Over the years, Jace had seen his fair share of just how nasty the world could be. Hell, he had the reminder tattooed on his skin, the image of a burning helicopter crashing behind them as he and a buddy pulled another soldier out. He'd gone to bed plenty of nights with grisly memories invading his brain and dreams. War was hell, and there were a plethora of monsters in the world, not just confined to children's stories.

Apparently sensing his agitation, Quinn moved closer. Laying a hand on his arm, she tipped her head back and looked up at him. Those pale brown eyes were so sincere. So open and trusting.

Too trusting.

"Warren is too intelligent to come after me. Right now his wife is reluctant to press charges, but I won't hesitate and he knows that. He has too much to lose."

He hated to burst her naive little bubble, but someone had to do it. "That's assuming he leaves you in a condition where charges are an option."

The dismissive sound through Quinn's throat did little to dispel his concern.

"He's mean, not stupid. Coldblooded murder is a far cry from backhanding his wife."

"Not that far," Jace muttered.

"Besides, at the moment his public image is safe, but it doesn't have to stay that way. He strikes me as the kind all wrapped up in appearances. He's worked hard to project the idea of an affluent, influential, *clean* business man."

Something dark crossed her face, a combination of anger and loathing. "He made damn sure to mark Caroline only where no one else would see." Her soft eyes rose to his, churning and resolute. "The bruises are bad enough. But she has burn scars across her stomach. And faint lines I'm almost sure are from him cutting her."

Spinning away, Jace shoved a hand through his hair. It was either that or slam it into the wall and he didn't want to have to repair the drywall. "You aren't helping me feel better here, Quinn."

"No, he's methodical and calculating. Polished and perfect. Yes, he's angry he lost his toy—"

"*You* took her and know exactly where he can find her."

"—but coming after me will only make matters worse. He isn't going to do that. He was throwing his weight around this afternoon because he could. Bluffing in the hope that I'd cave. That's all. If anything, I expect him to call in favors from some well-placed friends to put pressure on Daniel."

"Daniel won't give in." It wasn't a question. He'd been listening to Quinn talk about her job—and her boss—for two years. He'd gleaned several things, including that Daniel was a decent, upstanding guy who cared a great deal about the work they did and the people they helped.

But that didn't make this any less of a clusterfuck. He'd always worried about Quinn's job. She dealt with terrible things all day long—the emotionally draining, permanently scarring kind—and he didn't want that for her.

Unfortunately, she had a soft heart and a will of steel and wouldn't listen to anyone suggesting she find another way to make a living.

Her parents had fostered kids…at least, until the car accident that had killed them both. She'd grown up dealing with these kinds of horror stories. It was natural that she'd want to continue their work. And she was good at it.

Tomorrow he was going to pay Daniel a little visit, find out what he was doing to protect her.

Although, he was smart enough to keep that plan to himself. Quinn would just try to talk him out of it and there was no reason to fight her on it…yet.

"This is absurd." Quinn blew a frustrated breath out of her mouth.

"You're the only one who thinks so," Daniel said.

Behind him, Jace had his arms crossed over that

damn ripped chest. He tried to hide the smug smile teasing the corners of his mouth, but he couldn't quite pull it off.

She wanted to be angry with him for interfering, and she was pretty irked, but she knew he was only doing this because he was worried about her.

What pissed her off more was that he'd done an end run around her, going to Daniel behind her back. She could fight Jace, but not him *and* her boss.

Frustration and irritation buzzed through her brain. She felt the familiar rise of emotions, like a relentless high tide trying to erode her better intentions. Sure, she could let loose and spew anger all over Daniel and Jace, but that would just make her feel like a jerk.

"I don't have time to deal with this, Daniel, and you know it. My caseload is towering over me as it is."

"No one is asking you to ignore your work, Quinn. There are enough people in the office that you should be fine. We're more concerned with you being home alone at night."

She could see their point. The problem was that their solution was more likely to cause problems than the man they were afraid of.

"I will not be chased out of my own home. Especially not without a creditable threat."

Jace grunted, calling into question her statement with very little effort. She glared at him. He simply stared back, his clear blue eyes unwavering, until she couldn't take the direct connection and had to look away.

At least she managed not to blush. Her pale, freckle-ridden skin was a curse.

This was stupid and pointless. But she'd already said

that once, and they'd responded with the verbal equivalent of a pat on the head. Frustrating.

"I'll be staying with Quinn."

"You'll be what?" Quinn squeaked. "Don't you have, I don't know, a job?" she asked, her voice full of sarcasm.

Jace's mouth, already austere on a good day, pulled down into a frown. The dark line of his brows slammed together over a glare. No doubt the intimidating look was exactly what he used to keep the soldiers he trained in line.

Quinn had a feeling those men, given that expression, would jump to do whatever Jace Hyland wanted... right after wetting themselves. And it wasn't like Jace trained wussies. He had the best of the best, the strongest of the strong and the most masculine of the masculine under his command.

"I've taken some leave."

Okay, before she'd been miffed. Now she was royally pissed. "Because of this? Because of *me?*" God, she was going to hurt Warren—and then possibly Jace. This was getting blown out of proportion. Big time.

"No. I had this time off scheduled already for another reason."

Well, wasn't that just great. Why didn't that make her feel any better?

The man was on vacation—probably the first one he'd taken in two years—and he was sitting here preparing to babysit her as if she was a shaky-legged toddler.

"Why the hell aren't you on a sandy beach somewhere, then?"

He sucked in a breath. Quinn watched his chest expand and hold. She counted in her head, up to almost ninety before he let the breath go with a quiet rush that she felt deep inside.

"Not much on sand these days," he said quietly.

And Quinn immediately regretted her outburst. Who was she to tell the man how to relax? Her problem was, she wasn't sure Jace understood the definition of the word.

And if anyone deserved a chance to unwind and shed responsibilities, it was Jace. But that was a discussion for another time.

What she had to deal with right now was the threat of him moving into her home. It was hard enough to keep her mind where it belonged when he was in the middle of her office. Running into him in the hallway late at night? Quinn wasn't sure she'd survive the experience.

Not without embarrassing them both.

"There's nothing more important than this. I made a promise, one I intend to keep. Michael would never forgive me if something happened to you."

How was she supposed to counter that? Especially when his personal crusade was championed by a ghost. If she refused and, God forbid, something did happen to her, Jace would carry that guilt around with him for the rest of his life. He was weighed down with too much of that as it was.

This situation was spiraling out of control so quickly Quinn couldn't find a single slippery thread to grab so she could try to hold it all together.

Jace pinned her with his gaze. Her heart fluttered and a pressure settled right in the middle of her chest. He held her eyes for several seconds before saying in a low, fluid voice, "Humor me."

It wasn't a request, but he waited for her response

anyway. And for some reason, her ability to argue simply fled. She couldn't deny him. Not now. Maybe not ever.

Realizing her mouth had gone dry, Quinn simply nodded.

Aw, hell, what had she just gotten herself into?

3

"I COULD JUST stay here," Quinn suggested, despite knowing it wasn't going to happen.

Jace didn't even bother answering. He flashed her a cutting look and crossed his arms over his chest, waiting. Not very patiently.

A black bag sat on the floor beside him. His foot tapped, a staccato against the cool tile.

She'd discovered the reason he'd had leave scheduled. And she didn't like it. And really didn't want to go. Attending an MMA fight was more her idea of torture than entertainment. She'd never understood the draw, for men or women.

Brutality was something she fought *against*. And these men—Jace included—were embracing it. Training for it. Seeking it out.

She didn't understand and really didn't want to.

They'd been arguing for the past twenty minutes, though. It had taken her under five to realize Jace wasn't budging. She'd continued in the hope that eventually she'd make him late enough that he'd either leave her behind or, preferably, skip the thing entirely.

"In about thirty seconds I'm going to put you in the car myself. Stop stalling."

Or not.

With a resigned sigh, Quinn grabbed her purse and slung it diagonally across her chest.

The drive out was silent. A part of her was grateful for the residual irritation oozing between them and the distraction it provided. Inside her own head, she continued the argument, knowing it was about as productive as actually speaking the words out loud. But maybe her mental rant would drain the emotion away.

They pulled into a dark parking lot filled with cars and trucks of every make, model and price point. Jace's fingers brushed against her hip as he reached down and clicked open her seat belt.

Smacking his hands away, she snapped, "I can take care of myself, Jace."

Or maybe the brooding was just feeding into her already crappy mood.

He blew out a grim breath. Exiting, he went to stand at the hood of the car. Bag slung over one shoulder, his wide, hard back to her, he waited. Even in the early summer, it was already late enough to be full dark. Harsh light from a car in the spot three spaces over slashed across his forbidding body.

His silence said more than any words could have. And for some reason, Quinn had the urge to reach out and run a soothing hand over his tense shoulders.

Grinding her teeth, she fought back the instinct. Touching him always seemed to backfire on her, sending an unwanted tingle of awareness rushing through her body. Better to keep her hands to herself.

So, instead, she walked past him toward the rectangle of light spilling out into the night from the two huge doors propped wide open. Noise poured out, along with shouting, laughter and music. Apparently the fighting had started and there was already a match going.

She'd barely gotten through the doors when Jace's hand wrapped around her upper arm. Urging her forward, he directed her through the crowd, oblivious to the dirty stares that followed in their wake.

The dull roar of noise was a constant assault on her eardrums. Pulling her to a halt off to the left of the huge circular cage sitting in the middle of the room, Jace leaned down to speak into a guy's ear. The man, several inches shorter than Jace, flicked a quick gaze over his shoulder at her and nodded.

The man's eyes roamed up and down her body, not in a sexual way, but assessing. As if he was finally getting a look at a piece of artwork he'd been hearing about for years and was trying to decide if the hype was warranted.

Stepping away from the other man, Jace bent down to yell into her ear. She tried to ignore the soft puff of air against her skin and the tingle that chased behind it.

"Stay here. If you need anything tell Axe." He threw a glance over his shoulder at the guy still watching them. What kind of name was Axe? "Do not wander off, Quinn."

She huffed out a breath. Where the hell was she going to go?

"I'm serious."

Oh, she had no doubt he was. Having had just about enough of his overbearing, big-brother act, Quinn reached up, snagged the delicate edge of his ear and twisted until he brought it close to her mouth.

She didn't miss the way his lips twitched with suppressed humor. Or the wide grin stretching Axe's face. That did not help her mood. Okay, so maybe she pinched a little harder than she needed to. Part of her relished Jace's sudden intake of breath. The rest of her just regretted losing her patience and letting her emotions rule her actions.

"I doubt Warren decided to attend a local MMA fight on the off chance my self-appointed bodyguard—who he knows nothing about—was on the ticket tonight. I'll be fine."

She just wanted this to be over.

"Warren isn't the only threat, not here. There are plenty of dangerous men walking around tonight."

As if to punctuate his point, the heavy thud of bodies bounced against the metal of the cage a few feet away.

Quinn winced, recoiling out of instinct. Jace stood his ground, his only reaction a puckered frown.

The sickening sound of flesh connecting with flesh rang out, along with low male grunts. Quinn's gaze found the two men, tied together in a pretzel of arms and legs against the matted floor, as they tried to rip each other apart and force a submission.

Her stomach roiled. Blood trickled down the left side of one man's face. One guy squirmed uselessly against the hold of the other, his expression contorted with a combination of pain and resolve.

She had to look away from the spectacle, and was just in time to see Jace slip through a door several feet away. Until that moment, she hadn't realized he'd walked away. For some reason, it bothered her that he hadn't said anything before leaving her here, in the middle of all the bloodlust.

A hand slid down her arm. Her eyes wide, Quinn spun to find Axe standing behind her, pointing to an empty chair a few feet to the left.

Great. Maybe she could spend the next God only knew how many hours, surfing the internet and playing games on Facebook. She settled, angled her body as far away from the cage as possible, and pulled out her smartphone. But found she couldn't concentrate on anything except the sounds of combat ringing out around her.

It was like watching a train wreck. After a few minutes, she'd always find her eyes being dragged to the match. Better to see and know what was happening than let her imagination string together the grunts and smacks into some massive horror.

So far, none of the guys seemed overly injured by the time the matches ended. Sure they were bruised, and a few sported oozing cuts. But for the most part they all seemed happy to be involved.

By the third match, Quinn gave up the pretense that she was doing anything else. This wouldn't be her first choice for a Friday night, but since she had to be here...

That is, until Jace was announced. Suddenly, her heart was thumping like a speedboat motor. Something that closely resembled dread settled into the pit of her belly, churning and bubbling uncomfortably.

Sitting straight, Quinn gripped the edge of her chair. Lights flashed. Music played. And from the other side of the room, Jace entered the cage. His opponent made a show of his entrance, jumping up and grabbing onto the mesh. Rattling it, he yelled and the audience ate up his show of aggression.

Jace ignored him, calmly sauntering over to his corner and the men clinging to the cage on the other side. One of them spoke to him, although Quinn wasn't close enough to hear. Jace gave a single, sharp nod of agreement and then stared down at the floor.

She thought she saw him reach around and run his fingers along the tattoo covering his scars, but he was facing away from her so she couldn't be sure. A heavy band constricted her throat, making it hard to breathe.

Fear crawled up her spine, making her restless enough to stand for the first time all night.

Beside her, Axe shifted on his feet and eyed her, as if he expected her to do something stupid…like run. For a brief moment, she considered it, unsure she could stand there and watch Jace go through what she'd already seen.

But before she could do anything, the match started. Quinn held her breath, but that didn't last long. Especially when the first few seconds passed by relatively uneventfully.

The two men were fairly evenly matched, close in height and weight. They both had broad shoulders and defined arms. Thighs heavy with muscle flexed and contracted as they danced around the center of the ring. Every few seconds a fist would flash out like lightning, there and gone almost before she could blink.

Several minutes into the fight, Quinn's pulse finally started to settle. Her stuttered breathing evened. Her body relaxed, the grip she had on the back of her chair easing.

And that's when it happened.

Suddenly, his opponent slammed Jace up against the cage a few feet away from her. She watched the metal bow out under the weight of his body. Jace brought his arms up to defend his face, but that left the rest of him wide open. His opponent started whaling on him, landing body shot after body shot.

Jace fought back, connecting a few punches of his own. He writhed, trying to get out from under the weight of the body holding him in place. But he struggled as the other man's fists kept finding their mark.

She'd tried to block out the sounds of the fights all night, but suddenly Jace's grunts seemed like gunshots funneled straight into her ears. Each sound of pain lanced through her.

Panic seized her. Adrenaline shot into her system. She took a step forward, to do what she wasn't sure, but a heavy arm clamped around her waist, holding her in place. Someone screamed. It took her several moments to realize the frenzied words were tumbling from her own mouth.

She struggled, pushing against whatever was holding her in place. Someone had to stop this. She had to stop this. Stop it before he got hurt.

Dammit! The man only had one kidney. What if something happened? What if those body shots did permanent damage? What the hell had he been thinking?

What had his doctors been thinking, clearing him for this?

Quinn growled low in her throat. Of course, that assumed he'd bothered to ask.

Somehow Jace managed to force his way out from beneath his opponent and get back into the clear space at the center of the ring. Her body sagged with relief into the band still holding her.

A soft voice rumbled in her ear. "He's fine, *cielito*. The ref will stop the fight if he's in real trouble."

She shook her head, her lungs heaving hard. Held in place, she watched Jace take another hard shot to the face. His head snapped backward.

Quinn's eyes snapped closed. She couldn't watch. Pushing at the arm holding her she chanted, "Let me go. Let me go. Let me go."

Suddenly, the restraint was gone and she was free. For a second she stood there, suspended, unsure just exactly what she needed to do.

In the end she fled, putting the cage and Jace at her back and pushing through the crowd. She knew Axe followed her, could hear the complaints of the crowd behind her, but she didn't care. Couldn't care.

She needed air.

JACE BRACED HIS arms on his knees, his head hanging heavily between them. God, his body ached, especially his ribs. Although, the cut above his right eye also throbbed like a bitch.

He pulled a deep breath into his lungs, trying not to wince when his ribs protested.

He'd won, though a single moment of distraction had almost cost him the match. He'd looked up at one point and seen Quinn standing on the other side of the cage, her eyes wide with apprehension. In that split second, he'd found himself grasped around the waist and pinned to the cage, defenseless against the onslaught of fists and elbows and feet.

Stupid. He knew better than to leave himself open like that.

After that, he'd studiously avoided looking in her direction. He'd channeled all of his focus into the man trying to send him to his knees.

It was over. And for the first time in two years he was starting to think he was too old for this shit. Who would have thought thirty-one would be too old for anything? Certainly not him. But his body couldn't take the abuse it used to.

He'd found MMA by accident. When Michael had gotten sick and died, he'd needed an outlet. A safe release for all the pent-up anger, aggression and emotion. One of his buddies, a guy he'd growled at one too many times, had suggested he join a training program, not to compete but for the relief.

He'd fallen in love with the sport. The brutality and challenge of it. And maybe the reminder that he was still alive, his body functioning. It was getting harder and harder to remember why he'd needed the pain in order to feel connected to the world.

"Jesus, Jace." He hadn't realized Quinn was there until her soft voice touched him. Her words were followed by fingers slipping across his skin.

A sharp breath pulled through his teeth when she touched the cut over his eye—a combination of pain and twisting, unwanted need.

But she wasn't interested in soothing his hurts. Somehow he knew she wouldn't be.

Her palm cracked across his shoulder. Compared to the abuse his body had taken tonight, it was the equivalent of a raindrop in a hurricane. But unlike the other blows, he felt the echo of that harsh touch deep in his bones.

It rattled him as nothing else could. Not because it bothered him, but because any contact with Quinn always sent his body spinning out of control. Knowing she was upset with him didn't change that, although it probably should have.

He was like a starving man, willing to take whatever scraps were available. God, if Michael could see him he'd laugh his ass off. He was pathetic.

"Are you trying to die, too?" Her shrill words cut through him, more painful than his injuries.

"No." Although, he'd be lying if he said the thought hadn't crossed his mind.

Danger had been part of his life—his job—for so long, and he'd never hesitated to put himself in the line of fire, especially if it meant protecting someone else.

He'd been playing that role for years. Growing up, his father, a long-haul trucker, had been gone more than he'd been home. How often had he heard the words, "You're the man of the house"? By eight or nine, the responsibility of looking after his mom and brother was laid at his feet. And he hadn't minded. He'd liked knowing his father trusted him enough to take on the task. It had made him feel important. Like a man, though he'd been far from it.

But the mantle was difficult to shed, even after his father had retired and finally returned home for good. By then, he and Michael had been grown.

It was still hard to look his father in the eye whenever he dropped by to visit. He couldn't quite shake the feeling that he'd failed, miserably, by letting Michael die.

Ultimately, though, it was those same sad, tired green eyes—so similar to Michael's—that had kept him from doing something stupid. As much as it might have been easier on himself to push the envelope and take the easy way out with stupid risks, he couldn't do that to his parents.

Losing Michael had devastated them both.

Tonight it was all too much. He was just…tired.

With a sigh, he let his body sag into the physical exhaustion.

Quinn crouched in front of him. Her hands landed on his biceps, bracing her body. Heat he would have thought himself way too tired to feel surged through him. He shifted on the hard bench, trying to ease the sudden ache of having her so close.

Why was that pang so much sharper than all the others?

He tried to pull away, but she wouldn't let him go, clamping her fingers harder around his quivering arms. Ducking down so she could force him to look at her, she stared right into him. "Jace, you have to stop this."

He stared into her pale brown eyes. Wide, deep pools that threatened to pull him in and swallow him whole. Pressure suffused his chest, making it difficult to breathe. And suddenly he was angry. Pissed. At her. At himself. At Michael.

Throwing her hands off, Jace bounded up, temper snapping through him.

She rocked backward on her heels, startled by his sudden movement. Without thinking, he reached down and picked her up, steadying her even as he pulled her against his body all in one quick motion.

Her eyes widened, but she stood there, lax in his hold, flush against him.

His labored breaths brushed across her face, reflecting back at him.

"Don't tell me what I have to do, Quinn. You're in no position to cast stones. When's the last time you went on a date? Or even thought about another man?"

To his surprise something hot and sharp flared deep in her eyes, sparking through those golden flecks and flashing fire.

Her mouth opened, a small sound pushing past her lips. God, he wanted to drink it in. Which is why he let her go and took a step back. She stumbled, catching herself this time because he couldn't trust himself to touch her again.

Jerking her gaze away from him, she swallowed, and in a muted voice said, "That's different. I'm not hurting anyone."

"Only yourself."

Her soft, sad eyes found his again, the impact of them slamming straight into his chest.

Giving him a small shrug, she said, "Maybe, but I won't die from loneliness. You on the other hand..." Her voice trailed off to barely a whisper. "One wrong move in that ring and it could all be over."

Without waiting for his response, she walked away.

Sinking back onto the hard bench, Jace hung his head between his arms again. It was at least five minutes before he realized just what she'd revealed.

She was lonely. Alone. Just like him.

LAST NIGHT HAD been uncomfortable, although she was used to that sensation around Jace Hyland. Just as she had for years, Quinn had brushed it off and instead focused on life's mundane details. Making up the spare room. Getting him a towel and washcloth.

After she'd prepared everything, she'd retreated to the dark of her own room with the knowledge that Jace was next door—because he'd insisted on taking the closest room to hers in case something happened in the middle of the night. It had taken her several agonizing hours to fall asleep, her body restless and humming.

Although, when sleep had finally come, the relief had been short-lived, her dreams peppered with fantasies of Jace coming to her in the middle of the night. That gorgeous, sweaty, hard body sliding against her, into her, over her.

So she was awake early, groggy, grumpy and in desperate need of caffeine. Popping a pod into the coffee maker, she waited for the sweet, decadent nectar of the gods to flow through and into her cup. Less than sixty seconds later, the bitter scent of coffee laced with cinnamon, vanilla and caramel wafted up to her.

Taking a deep breath, Quinn closed her eyes and savored it for several seconds before letting the air out on a long, streaming sigh. Contentment settled across her shoulders. Cradling the hot mug in her hands, Quinn brought it close to her mouth but didn't drink. She'd learned not to sip unless she wanted to fight a burned tongue all day.

She waited, simply standing and staring down into the milky brown mixture in her cup.

This was her favorite time of day. Before the crazy started. Those first few easy moments. They never lasted long enough, so she'd learned to enjoy them when she had them.

Today the peace was shattered by the light shuffle of feet. Just as she had two days ago, she looked up to find Jace framed in the doorway to her kitchen, his arms stretched overhead and fingers curled around the door frame.

Jace's biceps strained the edge of the dark gray T-shirt with the print so faded she couldn't quite make out what it once said. The hem, worn so thin it was practically transparent, rode up a couple of inches to show a strip of darkly tanned skin.

He watched her with sleepy, mesmerizing eyes. Quinn took a quick sip of coffee—it was either that or blurt out something inappropriate—but she paid for the cover-up by scalding her tongue.

Yelping, she turned and spit the mouthful into the sink behind her. Jace shook his head and grumbled something about being careful before scooting past her. He didn't ask where her coffee cups were, just opened the right cupboard and pulled one down. He chose a pod—something bold and dark—and popped it into the machine. Reaching around her, he opened the fridge and pulled out her carton of milk. She never would have taken him for a milk guy.

What also surprised her was how easy he was in her kitchen, as if he'd spent lots of time there. She could probably count on one hand the number of times he'd been inside her home in the past two years. At least, with her here. It was obvious from his stint mowing her lawn the other day, and his helping himself to her kitchen, that this wasn't a one-time occurrence.

It annoyed her, but it also sent warmth splashing through her body. Which only increased her annoyance—with herself.

His coffee fixed the way he liked, Jace turned to face her, propping his lean hips against the counter. Crossing one bare ankle over the other, he studied her over the rim of his cup, his mouth pursed, a steady stream of air gusting out across the surface of his cup.

Dropping her gaze, Quinn took another tentative sip. One burn was more than enough for today.

They stood there in her kitchen, silently drinking. The air, heavy and oppressive, pushed in on her. It tightened her shoulders and made her skin tingle and itch.

One minute stretched into three and then five. She wanted to fill the silence, but had no idea what to say. So she just kept her mouth filled with swallow after swallow. Every few seconds her eyes would stray to him, not his gaze, but the rest of him. The long pants that clung to his hips and thighs. The curl of dark black hair over his ear. His strong fingers wrapped around the curved handle of his cup. Her cup.

Finally, when she thought she couldn't handle the tension for one second more, he broke the silence. "What are your plans for today?"

Flitting her eyes up to his, she took in the way he watched her and had to look away again. "Grocery shopping, a spin class. I'd like to run by the home-improvement store. I've been wanting to repaint the den for a while and the sink in the powder room has been dripping."

"Okay, just let me grab a shower and we can go whenever you're ready."

Shaking her head, she said, "You don't have to do that, Jace. It'll be boring as hell for you."

"It won't, but that's beside the point."

"Don't you have something more important to do?"

"Until I'm satisfied you're not in any danger, *you* are my number one priority. I'm not going anywhere, Quinn, so you might as well get used to having me around."

That was the problem. She'd been struggling against inappropriate feelings toward him for a long time. The only thing that had kept the urges in check was the infrequency of their contact…and the certainty he wasn't interested.

Having him constantly in her personal space, sleeping in her home and drinking her coffee…

She *could* get used to having him around. Quite easily. And that would be bad.

Jace and his parents were important to her. She didn't have a family of her own, not really. Her parents were gone. She and her sister weren't close and never had been. Tabby was seven years older than she was and had been in her freshman year at college when their parents died. Quinn had been raised by her grandmother.

There were other kids of all ages and backgrounds who'd revolved through the early years of Quinn's life. She'd always loved that her parents took in foster children, sharing their love and kindness with those who needed it most. But it had been years since she'd heard from any of those children.

She hadn't realized just how lonely she'd become until Michael's parents had made her part of their family. She didn't want to lose that simply because she couldn't control her baser urges.

A cup clattered into the sink, jolting Quinn from the dark turn of her thoughts. "I'm going to shower." Jace was halfway across the room before his body froze. Slowly, he turned back to her, pinning her in place with those clear blue eyes. He studied her for several seconds, his head cocked to the side. "Do not leave the house without me."

The thought hadn't even occurred to her, which made her a little angry with herself. But now that he'd mentioned it….

As if he could read the thoughts flitting across her

mind, his voice dropped down into a low rumble. "I'm serious, Quinn. If I have to chase after you neither of us is going to be happy about it."

Sighing, she nodded. Jace hesitated for a few more seconds, his gaze scouring her until he was apparently satisfied with what he saw. Quinn stood in the kitchen after he'd left, her body electrified and restless and unable to cope. But the sound of water rushing through the pipes galvanized her.

The last thing she needed was to stand here with her mouth open as visions of water flowing over Jace's naked body filled her mind.

Getting as far away from that end of the house as possible, she darted into the den. Popping open the drapes so sunlight could flood inside, she noticed several of the neighborhood boys in the yard between her house and the neighbor's, with a baseball and a bat.

A small smile curved her lips. The boys next door were nice, always yelling a hello whenever they saw her outside.

She'd just turned away, planning on filling the next few minutes with a brilliant con artist and his FBI handler on a recorded episode of *White Collar* when a loud crash startled her.

The scream that erupted from her throat was pure reaction. Glass shattered, tinkling to the floor in a shower of shards. A baseball bounced twice on laminate and then rolled. Loud, apologetic and panicked voices sounded outside her window. "Ms. Keller, we're so sorry! We'll pay for the window, promise."

On the other side of the window a handful of wide-eyed faces appeared. They were obviously alarmed by what had happened. But after the initial kick of apprehension and stutter of her heart, Quinn settled back. There were worse things in the world than a broken window.

"No worries, boys. It was an accident."

Walking around the broken glass—she'd take care of that after she retrieved a pair of shoes—she picked up the baseball from where it had rolled against the leg of her sofa. Popping it up and snatching it out of the air, she sent the cluster of faces a sly smile and a wink.

4

JACE WAS STANDING beneath the stone-cold stream of water, trying to get a handle on his libido, when a loud crash and high-pitched scream ripped through him as surely as any bullet could have. He knew the sound of terror when he heard it.

Chills that had nothing to do with the water rippled across his skin.

Quinn. He never should have left her alone.

Instinct and training kicked in. Slamming off the shower, Jace wrapped a towel haphazardly around his waist and bolted for the door.

Stopping only long enough to grab the gun he'd left in the bag in his room, he crept through the house. His senses strained for some sign or sound. Nothing. There was nothing. What the hell had happened?

It was probably less than ninety seconds before he'd swept the rest of the empty house and found himself in the last room, the den. And what he saw there left his skin clammy and made bile spin up the back of his throat.

The window was shattered, glass littered all across the floor. And the room was empty. Quinn wasn't anywhere in the house.

Had the bastard broken in and snatched her?

A flash of something off to the side of the house caught his eye. Dashing out the front door, Jace followed it.

The moment he saw her relief washed through him, stealing the strength from his muscles. Although that didn't stop his dash across the yard toward her.

He still had no idea which direction the threat was coming from and until he did...

"Quinn!" he called out, the single word harsh with warning.

She spun on her heels, eyes widening when she saw him barreling straight for her. Her eyes darted to the gun he pointed at the ground—he wouldn't raise it until he knew the target.

She shook her head, lifting her hands up and waving for him to stop. He didn't. Instead, he tackled her, wrapping his arms around her waist and rolling in midair so his body would take the brunt of the impact.

But he didn't stop when they hit the ground. That would have left her exposed. A soft gust of air swept across his cheek as her body collided with his. Jace kept rolling until she was pinned beneath him, his body becoming a shield.

Bent arms pressed by her sides, her palms flattened against his naked chest. He took a few precious seconds to scan her face and make sure she was unharmed before returning his focus to assessing their surroundings.

And that's when he noticed the five boys standing several feet away, gaping at them.

One of them, the oldest, held a baseball in his hand. Another had a bat. The others all held mitts.

An unpleasant thought twisted through his brain.

A frown pulling at the space between his brows, he growled, "What's going on?"

All of the boys shuffled backward a few steps.

"Jace, stop it," Quinn admonished. "The boys accidentally sent their baseball through my window. It was an accident, hardly worthy of a drawn firearm."

His gaze returned to Quinn. Her eyes stared up at him, exasperation and humor making those golden flecks sparkle.

Her body, tensed after his sudden assault, relaxed. She sank into the thick grass, unconsciously taking his full weight. Her fingers flexed against his naked skin. Her hips shifted. And suddenly he was hard as stone.

There was no way she could miss his reaction.

Slowly, the humor in her eyes faded, replaced with something much more dangerous...and tempting.

Her lush lips parted. Her fingers curled into his skin, as if to pull him closer. Jace's gaze fell to her mouth. Soft and pink. Full and enticing. He wanted to taste her. Wanted to know if she was as sweet as she smelled.

Had wanted it for a very long time.

His neck curved. Her chin tilted, moving to give him room. Her breath stuttered. They were so tightly pressed together, he could feel the hitch in her chest more than hear it.

Her eyes darkened.

But before he could actually claim her mouth, a small, hesitant voice interrupted.

"Uh, mister, you dropped your towel."

OH, DEAR LORD ABOVE.

Quinn's head turned slowly, her gaze traveling across the breadth of Jace's shoulders, down his tight biceps, still glistening with tiny droplets of water, to his large hand clenched around a gun.

Okay, so that definitely wasn't the hard ridge of his gun between them.

She sucked in a harsh breath, her body lighting up like the New York skyline on New Year's Eve.

"Uh, mister, you dropped your towel."

The high-pitched little boy voice had Quinn's gaze dragging back across the hard body pressed tight to hers.

She was human, after all.

It was her only excuse when her body curled up to sneak a peak of Jace's naked backside.

Dear, sweet heaven.

Her hands dug into the soft grass and tore it up by the roots. It was either that or grab a handful of him. As it was, she couldn't quite stop herself from squirming beneath him.

Jace hissed, almost like she'd hurt him. Panic surged through her. Had he injured himself diving to the ground?

That thought had her fists unlocking. They were so tightly pressed together, she couldn't see anything. But, oh, could she feel. Her fingers found his sides, running up over his ribs, down his hips and over the tight ridge of ab muscles, searching for some sign of damage. By touch alone, she explored him, pausing slightly when her fingertips brushed across the raised proof of the scars he'd tried to cover up.

Another groan rumbled up through his chest. The vibration of it shot straight through her, but she was too deep in worry to dwell on her reaction.

She searched his pale blue gaze, looking for any sign

of pain. And it was there, lurking deep in the back, an echo that sent adrenaline surging through her body.

"What did you do? Where does it hurt?"

Quinn wrapped her leg around his, and with a surge of her hips tried to flip him over onto his back so she could examine the rest of him. Unfortunately, the move didn't get her much of anything.

Jace's hips surged against her, driving her deeper into the ground and pinning her in place.

His long, lean body stretched over hers, reminding her that she could feel every hard inch of him. And there were plenty of them to feel.

"Really? Did you really just ask me that, Quinn?"

Heat flushed her skin, embarrassment and arousal.

"That's what I thought. Any idea where my towel went?"

As if by magic, a beige pile of terrycloth plopped down onto the ground right beside them.

Jace looked up, a grim smile curving his lips. "Yeah. Thanks."

"Sure," a voice said, clearly full of barely suppressed laughter. From a few yards away several snickers joined the moment. A battered pair of sneakers paused for a second before turning and retreating fast, followed by four more. They were blessedly alone, although Quinn wasn't entirely certain that was a good thing.

Rolling, somehow Jace managed to snag the towel, cover the strategic parts and end up on his back beside her on her lawn.

One arm plopped down over his face, shielding his eyes and expression from Quinn. Although she could see his mouth—his beautiful, kissable, tempting mouth—the corners crooked up in a smirk that hadn't fully formed.

Pulling her legs beneath her, Quinn sat up cross-legged next to him. Her knee brushed his hip. She should probably pull it away, but she didn't want to. She liked touching him. Liked the way any contact made her body buzz with an energy she hadn't felt in a very, very long time.

His chest rose and fell on even, measured breaths. And while the towel was draped across the middle of his body, it did nothing to hide the valleys and planes of his abs. Or the massive erection tenting the soft cotton. She'd seen him half naked last night, his shorts covering pretty much exactly the same amount of skin as the towel.

So why was she reacting like this was more?

"So, um, thanks for trying to save me?"

He rolled his head sideways, a single clear blue eye peeking out from behind his arm. "Sure. Any rabid baseballs, murderous footballs or wayward Frisbees attack and I'm your man."

Quinn reached for him, running her fingers down the slope of his arm in a gesture meant to soothe his wounded pride.

"It was sweet. Honestly. I know I haven't exactly been making this easy, but it means a lot that you're willing to put yourself in harm's way to protect me."

She had no idea what she'd said, but one moment amusement was lighting his eyes, the next his mouth tightened into a grim line and a cold shield dropped in place to cut her off from seeing anything else.

"Of course I'd protect you. You don't have to ask.

It's what Michael would have done. What I'll do since he can't."

For some reason, a large lump formed in the middle of her throat. It hurt, as though she'd tried to swallow a bite way too big.

He was wrong. Michael had been a lot of things—and she'd loved him for every one of them. He'd been a good man. But not the kind to charge into a dangerous situation, not caring about his personal safety.

Michael had been methodical and meticulous. He would have assessed the situation first. Calculated probabilities and then calmly called someone more qualified to tackle the problem.

Jace…he just went in with both barrels blazing. Damn the consequences. He thought she was in danger and that was all he needed to know in order to act.

Jace surged to his feet and Quinn watched him walk away. She got another brief glimpse of his delectable rear as he wrapped the towel around his body and secured it at his waist.

She didn't move, frozen in place, sitting in the middle of her front lawn as he walked away from her.

Pausing at her front porch, he didn't even bother turning back to her when he said, "You planning on sitting out here all day and entertaining the neighbors? Thought you had things to do."

THE REST OF the day dragged on endlessly. Everywhere she turned, Jace was there…along with the residual rumble of desire she couldn't seem to quash.

That moment on the lawn…something had shifted. Maybe not between them, but definitely inside her.

Sure, she'd been fighting fantasies of her almost brother-in-law for years. But now she'd felt him.

And knew he could respond to her. His body had definitely wanted her. And maybe it was simply rolling around with her on the ground that had done it. Maybe any woman he'd gotten that close to would have garnered the same physical response.

But her own body didn't give a damn.

Blocking out the urges was becoming more and more difficult.

They hit the home-improvement store, where Jace stood, arms crossed over his chest, and watched while she talked with a clerk and picked out paint. He didn't offer an opinion and she didn't ask him—although she was tempted, just to see his reaction as they discussed the pros and cons between harbor and kingfisher blue.

The only thing he did during the whole experience was gruffly suggest, "Get two rollers so I can help you."

She hadn't intended for him to spend his vacation protecting her—or painting her den—but she wasn't going to turn down the help. It would give them both something to do.

And maybe when they were finished she'd be tired enough that she could fall into bed and forget she'd started the day pressed tight against his hard body.

Although, their trip to the gym didn't help much.

She was grateful when Jace declined joining her spin class. Somehow she didn't see pedaling to nowhere as his preferred exercise. But the relief was short-lived when she walked out of the little spinning room, sweat pearling on her skin, to find him off to the side, a bar with an obscene amount of weight lifted high over his head.

Every muscle in his body strained with the effort.

For a minute, Quinn felt lightheaded. She had to reach out and grab onto a treadmill to keep from falling over. Too much exertion. And maybe her legs weren't completely back under her after pushing herself on the bike. That was it. Absolutely.

Her reaction had nothing to do with watching Jace's back, shoulders and thighs ripple with exertion.

Tipping the water bottle to her mouth, Quinn sucked a huge swallow down her suddenly parched throat. Forcing herself to turn away, she headed to the locker room. She normally showered at home, but today she was going to take fifteen or twenty minutes to get her head back where it belonged.

The day concluded with a very domestic trip to the grocery store. Since he was giving up his own plans to protect her—even if she didn't think she needed it— the least she could do was feed the guy. So she asked him what he liked and proceeded to fill the buggy with whatever he wanted.

It pissed her off when, instead of letting her pay, he pulled out his wallet and beat her to it. They argued in the middle of the checkout lane. The cashier, a woman in her early sixties who probably had several grandchildren, just stood there listening to them, the funniest smile on her face.

Quinn didn't understand why until Jace ended the argument by taking the buggy filled with bagged groceries and walking away, leaving her to finish the transaction and wait for a receipt.

"Y'all are the cutest couple. You remind me of my husband. We bicker over everything whenever he comes shopping with me." Folding up the receipt, the cashier handed it across the small counter separating them, but didn't let go. "Let me give you some advice. Let him do stuff for you. It's their ego. Makes 'em feel necessary."

Giving her a conspiratorial wink, the cashier sent her on her way. But instead of the sage words helping, they only ticked up Quinn's annoyance meter one more notch.

She was in a foul mood when they got home, everything building inside her higher and higher. The slam of cabinet doors was far from satisfying in bleeding off the churning emotions.

Jace ignored her temper, which didn't help at all.

His body was completely relaxed while Quinn was strung tighter than a drum.

Without another word, he disappeared out the back door. Pulling his shirt over his head, he threw it onto the table on her patio before cranking up her mower, picking up where he'd left off the other day.

Forcing her gaze away, Quinn channeled all her pent-up energy into cooking.

A couple of hours later she had a chocolate pecan pie cooling on the counter, a batch of garlic bread—she'd crushed the damn garlic herself—toasting in the oven and spaghetti sauce bubbling away on the stove. Not something out of a jar, but the recipe her grandmother had taught her when she was sixteen.

Even as the food heated, her temper cooled. Jace came inside and started banging around in her powder room, probably fixing the leak she'd mentioned in passing. Finally, she heard him settle into the den and the muted sounds of a ballgame filled the house.

Logically, she realized her reaction to everything had been out of proportion…probably more a result of her runaway libido than anything else.

The problem was, once cooled, her temper was no

longer operating as a buffer to the other things she didn't want to think about—or remember.

Like the feel of Jace's body sliding against hers. The welcome weight of his hips driving her into the ground.

The long, hard length of him.

He'd been aroused. The question remained, was it *her* or just a reaction to the circumstances? He had been naked, adrenaline no doubt surging through his body as he'd tackled her to the ground. Wouldn't most men react that way?

She wasn't sure. And it wasn't as if she could ask him. At least, not without feeling like an idiot.

Before Michael she'd had a couple of relationships— high school and college. Nothing serious, just friendly and fun. She wasn't a virgin and hadn't been for a long time. But she didn't exactly have a wealth of experience to draw from, either. She'd met Michael right out of college and they'd been together for a little over three years when he'd gotten sick.

It had been a very long time since she'd played the dating game. She was rusty and didn't trust her instincts where the signs of attraction were concerned.

Jace had never once given her the impression he thought of her as anything aside from an almost sister-in-law. That's what she told herself every time her mind wandered to places it shouldn't.

But what if she was wrong? What if he really did want her?

That doubt, that possibility, was what was driving her batty.

"Are you sure I can't help with anything?"

The low, rumbling timbre of his voice startled her. Quinn looked down and realized she'd been standing in front of the stove, holding up a spoon and staring as red sauce dripped back into the pot below.

"Uh…" She shook her head. "Why don't you set the table? This should be ready in about ten minutes, as soon as the pasta cooks."

They shuffled around each other, engaging in a sort of dance as they moved in and out of each other's way. She shifted left so he could reach around her for plates. He flattened against the counter so she could grab the strainer by his right hip. They moved silently, without communicating, as if they'd been doing it forever.

Unfortunately, it was all a lie. Because there was no comfort in the movements, only unacknowledged tension that relentlessly dogged them through the entire meal.

Somehow, they managed to fill the time with polite conversation; after all, they'd both had two years' practice making nice over dinner. But the longer they shared the same space the more brittle Quinn's restraint became.

It was just too much.

Unable to sit for one more moment without going mad, she pushed back from the table, the legs of her chair squealing out a protest against the floor. Gathering up the empty plates, she turned to the sink.

She had a dishwasher, but tonight she was going to hand wash every single plate, pot and pan. She needed the busywork.

Depositing the dishes, she turned to get the rest and slammed straight into a hard wall of male flesh. Her entire body rocked backward and every molecule of oxygen exploded out of her lungs on a whispered, "Oomph."

Slightly unsteady, she grasped for something to hold

her up. Her hands grabbed Jace's shirt, crumpling the soft cotton in her fists. Neck craned back, she stared up at him, eyes wide and mouth open like a fish.

Dishes clattered into the sink. Somewhere in the back of her brain she wondered if she was going to have to replace them all because they'd broken.

Strong fingers wrapped around her shoulders. They weighted her. Grounded her. Until that moment, she hadn't realized just how off-kilter her world had been spinning, until with a single, simple touch Jace Hyland somehow managed to yank her back to center.

"I'm sorry," he rumbled, his voice low and intimate. A shiver snaked down her spine. Warm heat puddled at the center of her body. It was delicious and comforting. She wanted more. Craved it.

Pushing up on her toes, Quinn let a single hand slip up over the contours of his shoulders to bury in the soft hair at the nape of his neck. She applied pressure, urging him down to meet her even as she rose to take what she wanted.

He made a wicked sound in the back of his throat, a cross between a whimper of pain and a groan of relief, when her lips brushed against his.

And then she was no longer in control.

Her feet left the ground. One of his arms wrapped beneath the swell of her rear and boosted her higher. Her body slid along his, delicious torture, as he aligned them perfectly.

He was hard, and this time there was no doubt, it was for her. She could feel the long ridge of him pressed into the softness of her belly.

His large palm cupped the back of her head. He urged her to move with him as he devoured her.

There was nothing soft about the kiss, but then, that wasn't Jace. He was hard and honorable, driven and all male. His tongue danced with hers, coaxing at the same time as he demanded.

Quinn whimpered, letting her neck fall back and her body arch into his hold. She was suspended above the ground, but she knew there was no way he'd let her fall. Ever.

Until he did. Although, technically, what he did probably couldn't be classified as dropping her. But it sure as hell felt as if he'd dumped her on her ass.

One minute he was kissing her senseless, the next his arms were gone and she was swaying on unsteady feet, blinking like a mole person being thrust into the light for the first time.

What the hell?

Taking several huge steps away from her, he ran his hands over his face. His fingers tunneled into his hair, tugging hard enough that Quinn winced and her own scalp tingled in sympathy.

Her chest rose and fell, her own breath whistling in and out of her lungs. Her brain and body desperately tried to catch up, but they were both sluggish, swamped with desire. It was like trying to turn a tanker on a dime—not going to happen.

She watched his eyes scrunch up tight and his entire face screw into an unhappy frown. Her stomach clenched at his expression, unease flooding through her. Not quite the reaction she'd been hoping for.

But what had her stumbling back, gripping the edge of the counter for support, was the expression in Jace's eyes when he finally dropped his hands and looked at her.

Guilt. Regret. Disappointment. Agony.

Definitely not the bliss still storming her own body.

God, what had she done? She'd started this, and instead of sharing something good with Jace, she'd caused him pain. More pain. Just what the man didn't need.

Her stomach turned, leaving a sour taste in the back of her mouth. Tears collected in her throat, a tight ball that burned.

But he beat her to the apology trembling on her lips. "I'm sorry, Quinn. That won't happen again."

He didn't give her the chance to accept or deny it. To promise him that this was all her fault and she was the one that wouldn't let it happen again. He didn't wait for her reaction at all, just spun away and left her there alone, clinging to the counter for support.

The entire house quivered with the impact as the front door slammed. Quinn whimpered.

Uncertainty and need mixed inside her.

Jace was obviously not happy about the kiss. She could see the regret stamped all over his face.

And she started to wonder if she should be feeling it, too. He was Michael's brother. Shouldn't she be feeling…terrible about touching him?

Guilty. She should feel guilty.

But she didn't.

And that, *that,* was what finally had the emotion surfacing.

5

SHE STOOD THERE, paralyzed with indecision. Run after him? Leave him alone?

After several moments her uncertainty became a decision all its own. Nothing. She was going to do nothing, the way she always did where Jace was concerned.

Turning back to the double sink, she filled one side with warm, soapy water and shoved in the pots and pans from dinner. Her mind whirled while her body got lost in the mundane task.

Until she glanced up at the darkened window that usually gave her a view of her backyard. With the glare of the light from the kitchen, it showed her only the black night…and a wavy reflection.

For a moment she thought Jace had come back inside. But her body didn't respond like normal. Instead of heat flooding her, a bone-chilling foreboding engulfed her.

The scream she wanted to let free strangled in her throat. Plunging her hand into the murky water, she searched blindly for the hilt of the dirty knife she knew was still hidden beneath the surface.

Relief burst through her when her palm closed

around the hefty weight of it. Sending an avalanche of grimy water surging with her, Quinn spun to face the man standing idly behind her.

Everett Warren.

He was entirely out of place, and not just because he didn't belong in her kitchen. His suit had probably cost thousands of dollars and was perfectly pressed, not a wrinkle in sight. She could practically see her reflection in the surface of his black, glossy shoes.

Warren's narrow mouth twitched into a sickly smile. Nodding at the knife, he said, "I've been standing here for several moments. If I wanted to hurt you I would have done it already."

His statement didn't stop the frantic pounding inside her chest. Her heart squeezed painfully. Even as adrenaline flooded her body, Quinn realized she needed to stay calm and rational. Think.

She scanned him as she tried to slow her racing thoughts enough to form a plan. His body language was relaxed, hands hanging at his sides. Empty. No weapon clenched in either fist.

Although, that didn't mean he didn't have one. Just not immediately trained on her.

Okay. Okay.

Forcing her lungs to expand, Quinn pulled in a deep, calming breath. Oxygen flooded her body and brain.

"How did you get in here?"

His mouth ticked higher into a twisted smile that held no humor. "I waited until your little bulldog slipped his chain. That was an unexpected development. Honestly, Ms. Keller, you didn't need to hire a bodyguard."

The smile dropping from his expression, Warren took a single step forward. Quinn thrust the tip of the knife in his direction in warning. He got it, stopping midstride and raising his empty hands in a gesture that was probably meant to be friendly, but didn't do anything to settle her nerves.

"I'm not here to hurt you, Quinn. I'd never do something like that. To you, Caroline or any other woman. I just wanted to talk to you. Try and get you to understand."

A bitter sound escaped through her tightened throat. "Oh, I understand." Anger was quickly replacing the fear that had settled over her skin like a nasty film. "I saw her, Warren. Not just the damage from the other night, but the scars. The ones you were so careful to only put in places she could keep hidden."

"Caroline's had a rough life. Yes, she was abused, but not by me. Never by me. I love her."

The sick thing was that Quinn believed him. It was there, shining out of his dark green eyes. He loved his wife, maybe a little too much if there was such a thing. But she could read the pain and desperation intertwined with the softer emotion.

Being without his wife was hurting him. The problem was, Quinn hadn't done that to him, he'd done it to himself.

"Even if that were true, that doesn't explain her new injuries."

Warren's head bowed, his gaze dropping to the tile beneath his feet. His entire body sagged. Reaching up, he ran his hands through his hair, and for a moment, Quinn's brain flashed to Jace giving her almost the exact same gesture not ten minutes ago.

His chest rose and fell on a defeated sigh, the sound so broken. Something twisted inside Quinn's chest, the empathy for anyone in pain that was inherent in her personality.

She took a step forward, ready to lay a hand on his slumped shoulder, and offer support and help.

Just in time, she caught herself.

Warren looked so crushed and mournful that Quinn found herself swallowing back a rise of answering emotion. But her training, and intuition honed on the job, told her to keep her distance.

"She's sick. Caroline's struggled with manic depression for years. Sometimes she stops taking her medication, especially when things are going well. Then she hurts herself. Maybe it's some twisted way to relive her past. Maybe she needs the pain. I don't know. The episodes have been getting worse and worse."

Tears glistened at the edges of his eyes. As she watched, several slipped free, trailing quietly down his cheeks.

"I just want to help her, Ms. Keller. I'm afraid of what she might do without the proper care and her medication."

He was good. The tears were a brilliant touch. And if she hadn't spent hours talking with Caroline, she might have believed his story. It wasn't outside the realm of possibility. She'd dealt with mental illness and the fallout before.

Which is also how she knew Everett Warren was full of shit. Caroline was as sane as anyone, which, considering what her husband had put her through, was actually a miracle.

Tightening her grip on the knife, Quinn said, "I won't tell you where she is."

As she watched, his expression morphed, a switch

flipped. The heartbroken husband disappeared, leaving behind a hard-eyed, shrewd and calculating monster.

This was the man she'd expected to see. The one who'd systematically abused and tortured the woman he claimed to love.

"We'll see about that," he growled. "I tried to do this the easy way, but you just won't give." A sickly smile twisted his mouth, glee flashed through his eyes before he managed to clamp it down. "So I'll make you."

Quinn was already scrambling backward before he'd taken a single step forward. Maybe if she could reach the back door she could escape into the night. Find Jace.

Find Jace.

The words pounded through her brain over and over again.

Her breath was harsh in her lungs. Labored. She needed to get a grip on herself or she wouldn't be able to run ten yards, let alone outrun this maniac.

For every step she took, he managed two. The gap between them was closing, but so was the space between her and the door.

Until he seemed to realize what she was intending and changed directions, cutting off her escape.

"Tsk, tsk, tsk," he said, waving a single finger in her direction. "You don't like to play nice, do you, Ms. Keller? Simply tell me where Caroline is and this ends right now."

"Not a chance in hell."

"Why would you put yourself in danger to protect someone you don't know?"

"Because she deserves a chance to escape from you, you monster."

He shook his head, genuine confusion beetling the

space right between his eyes. He really didn't understand how someone could be willing to sacrifice themselves to help someone else.

Complete narcissism. Quinn shouldn't be surprised, but she was. Because she really did believe that more than simple frustration at losing his toy was driving him.

The emotion when he spoke of Caroline was real… or as real as it could be for him.

Her avenue of escape cut off, Quinn had switched directions, trying to keep the bubble of space between them. Not until her back hit the edge of the island in the middle of the kitchen did she realize where she was. She'd been too preoccupied with keeping her focus on Warren.

Now she was trapped. Before she could scoot sideways, he was there, in front of her, blocking her way.

But he didn't touch her.

Maybe it was the knife she still held.

He simply stood there, staring at her, his head cocked to the side as if she was some oddity on display.

Her breath wheezed in and out, harsh to her own ears. Her fingers cramped, her grip on the knife handle was so tight.

It shook as she raised it into the space between them, pointed directly at the soft middle of his belly.

"Don't come any closer."

His gaze flicked down to the gleaming blade and then back to her, dismissing the threat in a way that sent chills racing across her skin. Why wasn't he worried?

Quinn stood there, poised on the precipice, realizing these could be her last moments on earth. Or at least, the last few without unbearable pain. She'd seen the evidence of just what kind of physical damage Everett Warren could inflict.

She almost wished he'd get on with it so she could at least fight. Despite having the knife, she couldn't bring herself to make the first move.

But it didn't happen.

Instead, the sound of the front door slamming blasted between them.

Warren jerked back, as if he'd just been slapped awake from a dream.

Spinning on his heel, he was halfway across the kitchen before Quinn could blink.

"We aren't through, my dear," he growled and then disappeared.

Quinn stumbled several steps, needing to feel empty space all around her instead of the hard press of counter closing her in.

She trembled, staring at where he'd just been, sucking in air.

GOD, HE WANTED to hit something. Preferably his own damn face, but since that was difficult to accomplish Jace settled for the support column holding up Quinn's front porch.

His knuckles burned at the impact, and unfortunately the torture didn't have the desired effect. It couldn't make him stop wanting her.

Although, Jace wasn't certain there was anything in this world that could do that.

He shouldn't want her. She was Michael's and off-limits for him.

She'd loved his brother. He didn't need to hear them recite wedding vows in front of friends, family and

God to know that. He'd seen it with his own eyes. The way her expression had gentled when she'd looked at Michael. The softness of her touch as she'd moved a sweaty piece of hair off his forehead.

Her broken grief when Michael had left them all.

Jace dragged a heavy breath through his nose, trying to clear out the lingering scent of her body. It didn't help, not when the taste of her still rolled across his tongue.

It was like ambrosia, a gift from the gods that he wasn't sure he'd be able to ignore now that he'd gotten a sample.

No. He was going to have to find a way back to before. Reaffirm his hands-off policy.

But every time he closed his eyes he could see her. Passion staining her skin pink beneath the dusting of freckles. The way her beautiful brown eyes had gone unfocused even as she'd stared up at him, golden flecks flashing fire.

She'd started the kiss, but he'd taken something she'd probably meant as soft and easy, friendly, and twisted it with his own heat and need.

Even then she'd been with him, every step of the way. Which only made what he had to do now harder.

Quinn was lonely. He'd seen it last night at the fight, recognized the hollow emptiness inside her because he had a matching black hole sucking at his own chest.

But that didn't mean she wanted him. He was convenient and comfortable, nothing more. She'd have reached out for anyone.

He couldn't be the one to help her move on, not without losing her completely when the physical need had passed. Eventually she'd crash back to reality, take one look at him and see the man she'd lost.

And he didn't think he could handle the crushing blow when that happened.

Pulling in one more steadying breath, Jace paced across the porch. He bounced on the balls of his feet, welcoming the familiar way his muscles warmed beneath the action. He let muscle memory take over, arms flashing out in quick succession, jabbing at blank air and giving his mind something else to concentrate on.

Ten minutes later, sweat was popping out across his forehead for a very different reason than his body had expected. But he felt more in control. At least enough to go back inside.

What he didn't expect to find was Quinn standing in the middle of her kitchen, her face ghostly pale, her freckles popping out from her skin. She was shaking, a fine tremble wracking her from head to toe.

"What the hell happened?" Jace asked, searching for the source of her fear even as he bounded across the room to her. Because it was clear from the vacant expression in her eyes that she was scared spitless.

Slowly, she turned. For the first time he realized she had a death grip on a knife. It clattered to the floor at her feet.

He didn't know what to do. What was wrong? A sickening sense of helplessness dropped into the pit of his stomach.

Without thinking, he reached for her, gathering her into his arms and sheltering her with his body. She buried her head in his neck, sinking in and letting him hold her. And some of that restless energy began to fade. Until her muffled words reached his ears. "Warren. Was here."

Every muscle in Jace's body went rigid. "Here? Just now?"

Quinn nodded. He swore, long and low, beneath his breath.

Placing a hand on either side of her face, Jace eased her head back so he could look into her eyes. "You're fine. You're safe. Where did he go?"

She licked her lips, shaking her head. "He left. Out the back door."

He hooked the leg of a chair with his foot and pulled it out until it touched the back of her legs. Easing her down, he crouched in front of her, wrapped her hands in his and placed them in her lap. Ducking so he could snag her gaze, he said, "Stay here."

He didn't like leaving Quinn, but he didn't like being unarmed more. Striding down the hall to his room, he pulled out both of the handguns he'd brought with him. They were loaded and ready to go. Tucking the Glock into the waistband of his jeans, he checked his .22 anyway, flipping off the safety and then putting it back into place.

Returning to the kitchen, he opened Quinn's palm and placed the gun in it, wrapping her fingers around the grip.

She resisted, trying to push him and the weapon away. "No. I don't want—"

"Quinn, I have to go outside and check to make sure he's gone. I don't want to leave you alone in here unarmed."

Quinn's gaze strayed to the knife sitting several feet away on the floor. Slowly, she nodded. "But I don't know how to shoot," she whispered.

"Doesn't matter. If he comes back just point it at him

and fire. Hitting anything will slow him down and probably have him scrambling for cover, at least long enough for me to get back to you. I won't be far."

She nodded, her lips pale and bloodless, but beneath the telltale signs of stress there was a resolve he admired. Quinn was tough and always had been. He'd seen it time and again as she'd stood at Michael's side, his rock through everything.

Quinn had nerves of steel. She tackled problems head-on, including this.

Leaving her sitting there was one of the hardest things he'd ever had to do, but logically he realized securing the perimeter was more important. Better late than never.

The thought had his stomach filling with the heavy weight of regret. There'd be time enough for self-recriminations when this was finished.

Jace slipped into the night. Now he taught others how to blend into the darkness and assess surroundings for evidence of a threat. He'd be lying if he said there wasn't a small part of him that relished the rush of adrenaline pouring into his system.

If the source of that were anything besides danger to Quinn he'd have been in seventh heaven. But since it did involve her…

He didn't bother turning on the outside lights, preferring the cover darkness provided, although it helped the enemy just as much as it aided him.

In a widening circle, he rounded the house, checking for any sign that Warren was still out here. He didn't think the man was stupid enough to stick around, but then he'd been half convinced by Quinn's arguments that Warren wasn't stupid enough to do anything at all.

After five minutes he'd combed every inch of her yard and the neighbors' yards on both sides. There was no sign of the man—or anything to indicate how he'd gotten in and out without notice.

Walking in the back door, part of Jace was proud to look up and find Quinn still sitting where he'd left her, but with the barrel of her gun pointed straight at him. It didn't waver for several seconds before she dropped her arms and let it fall back into her lap.

At least her skin had lost the ghostly pallor.

Striding over to her, Jace eased the gun out of her hands and laid it on the table beside her. Bracing his hands on the arms of the chair, he looked down at her. Her head dropped back against the rounded curve as she watched him.

"Let's get you packed."

He'd expected to rehash the same argument they'd had yesterday when she'd refused to leave. It was clear by the quick glitter that shot through her eyes that she wasn't happy about the situation. But at least she was smart enough to realize the intelligence of leaving, now that they knew Warren could—and would—get to her.

With a tight nod, she moved to stand. Her body brushed against his, sending him straight back to red alert.

Taking several huge steps back, Jace gave her the space to scoot around him. She headed down the hall, hopefully to pack.

He stayed right where he was, hands tightened into fists at his sides.

They'd shared her three-bedroom, two-bath house for less than twenty-four hours and he'd nearly lost his mind, kissed the hell out of her and let his own libido chase him away and leave her vulnerable.

How the hell was he going to handle moving her into his tiny apartment with only one bed? Here they'd had a little space.

There…they'd be crawling over each other.

His rock-hard erection thought that was just a jim-dandy idea. At least his brain realized he was setting himself up for more torture than relief.

6

QUINN CONTACTED A LAWYER and began the process to file a restraining order. Having legal paperwork in the system would increase the chances of being able to do something if Warren messed with her again.

The flip side was that she was publicly tarnishing Warren's reputation. And he'd pulled the wool over quite a few well-connected eyes. No doubt, he'd know she'd made the request before the ink had dried.

And while that really didn't bother her, she had enough experience with men like him to realize it would only make him angrier and more dangerous.

But she'd have to take that chance. The man would not intimidate her.

That just left settling into her temporary home.

In all the years she'd known Jace, she had never been to his apartment. Quinn wasn't sure what she'd expected, but it certainly wasn't the cat that greeted them at the door.

The fluffy, flat-faced cat bolted toward them, winding around Jace's legs and meowing loudly. She looked up at him, love and adoration clear in her bright blue buggy eyes.

She was absolutely adorable. The kind of cat any self-respecting five-year-old little girl would go goo-goo over. The only thing she was missing was a pink satin ribbon tied around her neck.

Not exactly army-badass material.

"I, uh, never took you for a cat guy," Quinn said, trying to suppress the laughter choking her.

Jace eyed the cat for several moments and then transferred his glare of disgust to Quinn.

"I'm not. Bacon broke into my apartment. Hid under my bed, the couch, above the kitchen cabinets. I put her out again, but for weeks every time I opened the door she slipped back inside. I got tired of chasing her around the apartment and just…let her stay."

Quinn didn't know which part of his statement to tackle first, the part where a tiny fluff ball of a cat had outsmarted him, or that he'd named her after cured meat. Better not to point out the hit to his masculinity.

"Bacon?"

"Yeah. I haven't eaten a piece since she moved in six months ago. Somehow she manages to snatch it right off my plate. Apparently, it's her favorite."

Smothering a snort, Quinn walked away. It was either that or laugh hysterically in his face, and she didn't think that would be good for anyone.

Her gaze ran over his apartment. Yes, the space was small, but it was…cozy. Comfortable. On random surfaces she noticed photographs—several of his parents and Michael. A couple of him and Bacon. She wondered if a girlfriend had taken them and tried not to care.

Walking closer, she took in a group scattered across

a bookcase shelf. Candid shots, including a few with her, from Christmases, birthdays, Saturdays gathered together to watch football. Seeing them had a bolt of sadness lancing through her.

But it was the photograph tucked behind the others that broke her heart. One she'd never seen before, the edges turning yellow with age even through the protective gleam of glass. Michael, a huge smile stretching his mouth and lighting his eyes, laughed directly into the camera. He was young, probably in high school if she had to guess, but she could see glimpses of the man she'd loved.

Beside him, an arm wrapped tight around Michael's shoulders, stood Jace. He wasn't joining in the laughter. Instead his face was intent, his gaze trained solely on his brother. She'd always known Jace looked out for Michael, but this picture illustrated the concept beyond a doubt.

Looking at it made her heart ache, and not for the reasons she'd expected. Michael's smiling image stirred fond feelings, but she hurt for Jace. For what he'd lost.

And then she felt guilty about it. Not for caring about Jace, but because he was her main concern, not the man she'd lost.

When she looked at the photographs of Michael she no longer thought about the life they should have had.

When had that happened?

Quinn wasn't entirely certain how to feel about that realization.

What she did know was that the photograph was beautiful. It bothered her that it wasn't front and center, but tucked out of the way. Reaching in, Quinn shifted the rest of the frames around until it was prominently on display.

She turned to find Jace watching her, that same intense expression from the picture now trained on her. A little older. A little more haunted. But still...the same. His gaze traveled over her shoulder and lingered on the photo for several seconds before returning to her.

His expression was enigmatic. The man was difficult to read on a good day, and this one had been far from good. She waited, mostly for him to say something to her about messing with his stuff. But he didn't.

Turning on his heel, he headed down the darkened hallway and pushed open one of three doors. "Bathroom's through here, just clear off whatever space you need. Towels are under the sink." Passing by another door on the left he pointed. "That's my office. Not much in there other than a desk, computer and some random junk."

Pausing outside the last door, Jace pushed it open and stepped out of her way. She got her first glimpse of his bedroom. It was just like him, a little austere but with glimpses of warmth.

The walls were painted a rich, warm brown that, for some reason, reminded her of sitting around a campfire, making s'mores and licking melted chocolate from her fingers. Instead of a spread, a handmade quilt covered the bed. Quinn recognized his grandmother's work. She wasn't with them anymore, but the family cherished her talent and passed down the quilts. Quinn had tried to return Michael's quilt after his death, but his mother had insisted she keep it.

It was sitting on a shelf in her hall closet. At the time

she hadn't been able to look at the beautiful quilt without crying. Now she was regretting tucking it away.

Walking inside the room, she paused to run her hands over the tiny, perfect stitches. It was soft and no doubt warm on chilly winter nights. There was a part of her that loved Jace for actually putting it on his bed.

It wasn't the kind of thing you'd expect from a big, macho military man. But then, Jace wasn't your typical anything.

The furniture all matched, a deep cherry wood. The top of the dresser was completely bare, with not a single speck of dust marring the finish. On the far wall a line of shoes and boots marched toward the corner.

It smelled like him. Something smooth with a tang of spice and an edge of pure male.

Slowly, Quinn turned back to where Jace had stopped just outside the door. Once again, he reached overhead holding onto the frame and making the muscles in his arms ripple up and down.

"You take the bed. I'll sleep on the couch."

"No. I'm not kicking you out of your room, Jace." That's where she drew the line. He was already disrupting his entire life for her, she'd be damned if she let him do any more.

"I'm not arguing with you about this, Quinn. Take the damn bed." His eyes flashed a warning.

Emotion bubbled up inside her, hot and hard. Even as the volatile mix churned up the back of her throat, she realized the anger and frustration and fear and guilt and lust and just…everything had little to do with Jace's hard-line stance on the bed issue.

That didn't stop the words from spewing out of her mouth.

Stalking across the room, Quinn smacked his chest with her palms. He rocked back to his heels, but didn't go far. Which didn't do much to help her writhing temper.

"Jace, stop telling me what to do." The heat of all that bottled-up emotion burned across her skin. She could feel it, caustic and destructive. "I'm a big girl and I don't need a keeper."

His only response was a matching flash of temper that ripped through his annoyingly clear and mesmerizing eyes. However, his words were low and measured when he responded, "Obviously, that isn't quite true, now, is it?"

Quinn sucked in a hard breath.

"None of this is my damn fault."

"I don't remember saying it was."

His hands slid down the wooden door frame separating them. His knuckles, still a little tattered from the fight, turned white. He was trying to hold on to his temper.

What did it say about her that she wanted him to let go? She'd never, not once, seen Jace wild with emotion. Not even when Michael took his last breath. Inside that tiny room where they'd brought him for those last few hours, Quinn had completely lost it.

She'd held it together in front of Michael, but once he was gone she'd become a sobbing, hysterical mess. His mother had been just as distraught. His father had been quieter, but still racked with grief.

Jace had stood silent and stoic. She could still remember the supporting weight of his arms holding her up.

She'd wanted him to scream at her, God, Michael, fate. But he wouldn't. Not then. Not now.

It frustrated her. Fueled her anger even more. Made her grit her teeth and just…

Slowly, reality returned, the red haze of her emotions bleeding dry. Quinn realized her breath was coming fast and shallow. She stared up at Jace, guilt and regret settling hard across her shoulders.

They bowed beneath the weight.

God, this whole damn mess was turning her into someone she didn't like or want to be.

Shaking her head, Quinn took a step back, trying to move away from Jace and her outburst.

"Feel better?" he murmured.

Folding onto the edge of the bed, she dropped her head into her hands, covering her eyes with the heels of her palms.

"Not really," she replied, her response muffled and full of regret. Sucking in a deep breath, she held on to it for a second before finally letting go.

Suddenly, warm hands covered hers, gently tugging until she had no choice but to let him move her hands away from her eyes.

Crouched at her feet, he stared at her, his gaze more soft and gentle than she'd ever seen it.

That did not help the guilt swirling inside her. It only made her hate herself more that she hadn't been able to control the outburst.

"Hey, cut yourself some slack, Quinn. You've had a crappy couple of days."

"Maybe, but that doesn't mean I should take it out on you."

His broad shoulders lifted and then dropped. "Why not? I'm here. I can handle it."

"Doesn't make it right."

Humor tugged at the edges of his lips, pulling them into a lopsided grin. His eyes began to glitter in a way that had her breath catching in the back of her throat.

"Well, if you really feel bad about it, I know exactly how you can make it up to me."

There was some resemblance between Jace and Michael. They had the same dark hair. The same almond-shaped eyes. The same deep laugh, not that she'd heard Jace's very often.

But there were more differences than similarities. However, in that moment, Jace's face stamped with the same impish grin she'd seen so often on Michael, there was no doubt the two men were brothers.

Her fingers tingled with the desire to reach out and touch the curved edge of his mouth. She wanted more than anything to kiss him.

But was that because he was being sweet or because he suddenly reminded her of the man she'd lost?

Somewhere she found the words to keep their conversation going, even if her brain was in meltdown mode. "Oh, yeah, what's that?"

Pushing up from his crouch, Jace towered above her. She had to crane her neck to look at him, her eyes enjoying the long stretch of masculine perfection on the way up.

"Take the bed."

Suddenly, she was just…exhausted. Mentally, physically, emotionally drained. "Oh, whatever. But only if we take turns. Tomorrow I get the couch."

His mouth twitched, but all he said was, "We'll see."

She sat there for several minutes after he walked away, listening to him move around the apartment. The soft pad of his feet over carpet. The clang of something in the kitchen. A door opening and closing. She wondered what he'd sleep in, because he certainly hadn't taken the time to grab anything from the dresser.

Finally realizing what she was doing—and the effect it was having on her body—Quinn bolted up from the bed and scrambled across to her bag. It took her ten minutes to get changed, wash her face and brush her teeth. And less than that to realize she should have fought harder for the couch.

Cocooned in the darkness, underneath the weight of his covers, the only thought running repeatedly through her brain was that she was in Jace Hyland's bed.

Alone.

How many times had she entertained illicit fantasies of being right here? More than she cared to admit—even to herself. But none of the scenarios had played out like this. Surrounded by his scent, his things, she was utterly and irrevocably alone.

An ache centered in the middle of her chest. Another twinged hard between her thighs.

Screwing her eyes shut, Quinn started counting sheep. Anything to occupy her brain with something aside from what she wanted and couldn't have.

She was usually one of those people who dropped right to sleep minutes after her head hit the pillow. Not tonight. She tossed and turned, dozing for a few minutes at a time before jerking awake.

Finally, unable to take anymore, her spent body took over and plunged her into sleep. But the restlessness and the stressful events of the past few days conspired against her.

THERE WAS NO way he'd have let Quinn take the couch. His mama had raised him better than that. But every time he closed his eyes a vision of her stretched out in his bed tattooed itself on the inside of his lids.

Even after this was over, he'd never be able to look at his bed again without thinking of her there. Maybe he should have taken her to a hotel. The price of a suite with separate bedrooms probably would have been worth it for his long-term sanity.

Jace was used to going without sleep. His body had been trained to withstand harsh conditions and operate on nothing more than a few stolen moments of shut-eye here and there.

Pillowing his head on his arms, he stared up at the ceiling of his den, watching the shifting shadows as outside clouds moved across the moon.

A heavy weight settled on the center of his chest. Bacon kneaded her paws against him, purring even as she rubbed her furry face beneath his chin. His skin itched, but he didn't make a move to shift her off.

For once, he appreciated her company.

It was going to be a long night.

If he didn't need to stay sharp in order to protect Quinn, he might have caved and pulled out the bottle of scotch sitting in his liquor cabinet. But since that wasn't an option, he'd put the time to good use coming up with a solution to Quinn's problem.

The soldier in him wanted to call in a tactical team, devise a plan of action and move in to take the man out. With his bare hands, if necessary.

The rest of him realized that wasn't viable, though it frustrated him that his hands were tied.

So all he was really left with was keeping her safe. Even if that meant protecting her from herself. Although, perhaps Quinn was finally willing to admit she was in real danger. It was obvious that having Warren barge into her home had upset her and left her more than a little shaken.

Good, she needed to take the threat seriously.

He had another week of leave already scheduled. If push came to shove he could ask for more. But she couldn't live under the constant strain. He knew Quinn well enough to realize she *wouldn't* live under the constant strain.

The woman was fierce and determined. She didn't let anything faze her, something he admired quite a lot. She insisted on standing on her own two feet, to the point of frustration when someone wanted to help. She bent over backward to take care of those in need, blatantly disregarding the cost to her own safety and sanity.

She was admirable, although that didn't stop him from fighting the desire to take her away from it all so she never had to see or experience anything difficult again.

Quinn Keller deserved the easy life. But she didn't really want it.

His need for her went far beyond the physical, although there was no denying he wanted her. And the longer they were together, the harder it was to suppress the basic, animalistic urge to claim her as his own.

Kissing her hadn't helped. That one taste…never enough. And earlier. The way her skin had flushed with pique and her eyes had spit venom at him…she'd been amazing and all he'd wanted to do was give her a more pleasurable outlet for the churning emotions tormenting her.

He'd realized immediately that she wasn't really angry with him—well, she was, but that wasn't where her temper had come from. He'd seen enough responses to stressful situations to realize it was a delayed reaction.

He'd thought briefly about offering his body for her to use instead—if only as a punching bag—but had decided that was just taking things too close to the line he couldn't cross.

Even now, hours later, his body was still responding to her, alive and pulsing with the urge to stand up, walk down that hallway and claim what he'd wanted for so long.

Jace clenched every muscle, drawing tight before forcing the tension back out again. And he stayed right where he was, feet hanging off the end of a couch that, while large, was never designed to accommodate a guy his size.

He must have finally dozed, because one moment he was forcing his mind away from Quinn, warm and languid in his bed, and the next he was bolting upright. Off balance, he crashed to the floor with a clatter loud enough to wake the downstairs neighbors.

He was disoriented, but the gun he'd placed on the coffee table was in his hand before his brain had a chance to catch up and assess.

A whimper slipped down the hallway, making his heart clench. It was a wounded animal sound, choked tears and a strangled cry.

Could Warren have found them?

No damn way.

They were on the fourth floor and the only way into the apartment was past him. Even if he *had* been asleep, he would have woken up if someone had broken in.

Dashing down the hallway, Jace had a brief flashback to yesterday morning and his headlong charge out of the house in nothing but a towel. At least tonight he was wearing boxers. But maybe he should check things out before assuming the worst.

The door to his room was open a few inches. Leading with the barrel of his gun, he eased it open the rest of the way.

The sight that greeted him had panic surging through him, but not because Quinn was in any real danger.

Through the darkness, he watched her body thrash beneath the covers. Her limbs were tangled in the quilt, her right leg and left arm out while the rest of her wrestled as though she was being smothered.

She moved, flashing him the inside of her thigh, her skin gleaming in the faint light from the hallway, and he realized she was sleeping in nothing but a loose T-shirt and panties.

Need shot through him, held back for too long to be easily contained, mixing with the adrenaline pumping into his blood. Jace stumbled, grabbing the edge of the dresser to keep himself upright.

Her eyes were shut tight, her face screwed into a mask of terror and grief. For the first time he noticed the glitter of tears tracking down her cheeks.

She made another sound, her entire body bowing up off the bed as if the tortured howl had been torn straight from her soul.

He tossed his gun to the dresser, and it made a loud clatter as he leaped across the room. Jace freed her from the covers, tearing them off her and throwing them to the end of the bed. Collapsing beside her, he gathered her into his arms and tucked her body close.

She shuddered.

"Shh, you're safe. I've got you," he whispered directly into her ear. One hand rubbed rhythmically up and down her back as the other smoothed damp strands of hair away from her face.

She sucked a heavy breath in through open lips, held it for several seconds and then let it go in a long, steady stream that seemed to drain the tension away.

Her eyelids fluttered, as if her body was reluctant to throw off the last dregs of whatever nightmare had pulled her under. After a few moments, though, she won, her eyes finding his.

"Jace?" she asked, her voice shaky and raw.

"Yeah."

"What are you doing here?"

"You were having a nightmare."

She dragged in another unsteady breath. "Oh."

He expected her to pull away, consciousness stealing the comfort he wanted desperately to give. Instead, she seemed to melt into him. Warmth spread through him, accompanied by an edge of fire that he ignored. Or tried to.

Reaching up, she rubbed her hands across her face. Her words were muffled, but he heard them clearly enough. "I haven't had that nightmare in a long time."

That nightmare. Not a nightmare, but one that she'd dealt with before.

"Tell me about it."

His body was already stiff from trying to sleep on a torture device parading as a sofa, but it didn't matter. He leaned against the headboard, not caring that it was hard on his back.

Shifting Quinn, he lifted her legs so she was draped across his lap. Her hands settled over his shoulders and her face found the crook of his neck. He could feel the soft brush of her breath against his skin.

The tiny hairs on the back of his neck stood on end. "It's the crash that killed my parents."

He knew they'd been killed and that she'd been in the car, as well, but he'd never gotten any real details. Asking had seemed like the wrong thing to do, requesting information he didn't have the right to possess.

Now…now she needed to talk through the nightmare.

"I remember everything about that night. We'd been out all day, at one of those Renaissance festivals a few towns over. I'd had a great time, but too much fair food had made my stomach hurt. I was laid out on the backseat trying not to get sick everywhere. Halfway home, out of nowhere, it started to rain. Hard. In minutes I couldn't see anything outside the window, but I was too young to realize that meant my dad—and any other drivers on the road—couldn't see, either."

Her eyes, normally so bright with life, had taken on a far-off expression that had his stomach churning. Sadness weighed on her, as heavy as the blanket piled into a heap at their feet. He wanted to wash it away for her.

"I guess he didn't see the car coming until it was too late." She shrugged. "God, I hope that's true. Even a few moments of knowing would be too much. Witnesses said the car that hit us hydroplaned, spinning out of control and slamming into us."

Another shudder wracked her body. Jace felt helpless. Useless. He opened his mouth to tell her to stop, that if reliving the night hurt her that much she should just stop. But she didn't give him a chance to actually voice the words.

"Without my seatbelt, I was thrown to the floor. They tell me that's what saved my life. The front of the car crumpled in. Somehow, the other car went airborne, crashing across the roof of ours before tumbling off again to rest behind us. I just remember the god-awful sound. Screeching metal. My mother screaming by name and then…silence. Rain pinging off the windows. My legs wet.

"Somehow I crawled out. I was standing on the side of the road, just staring at the wreckage when the rescue teams arrived. I had a few cuts and bruises, a concussion. My parents were so battered we couldn't have open caskets. And the other driver…"

She swallowed, her eyes screwing shut for several moments.

"The horn on that damn SUV wouldn't shut up. It just kept going, but it didn't sound right. Broken, but refusing to stop."

Just like Quinn.

She'd been battered over and over again. Losing her parents. Losing Michael. Her job kept her knee-deep in the worst humanity had to offer. But she just kept going.

Jace envied her. In that moment, he realized just how mired down he was. How stuck in the past and driven by what he couldn't prevent.

"I was so angry for so long." She laughed, the sound tinged with a hint of bitterness. "My poor grandmother came pretty close to disowning me. I lashed out. Refused to listen to anyone. Got into trouble. Until I was forced into a counseling program at my school. It was either that or get expelled."

"What the heck did you do?"

Her large, lush mouth curved up at the edges. "What didn't I do? Short of calling in a bomb threat, you name it, I did it. I was too young to realize my actions were a cry for help, my anger and pain twisting me up inside with no outlet. But I worked hard over the years to control my temper, to try to channel it into something productive. Although I don't always succeed. And so far, over the past couple of days, I'm pretty much batting zero."

He couldn't keep his fingers from smoothing down the slope of her shoulder. Across her soft skin. Offering the only form of comfort he could. Because nothing could change what had happened to her parents.

"Michael never told me," he finally whispered.

"Why would he? I never told him."

Jace's arms tightened around her. "Why not?"

She snorted, the sound so perfectly wrong. "Really? We both know Michael was perfect. I honestly don't think the man ever suffered from self-doubt."

"He would have understood."

"He would have tried. But it's the difference between sympathy and empathy. I'm not ashamed of my mistakes. They made me the person I am and most days I'm pretty happy with me. But…" She shook her head.

A single question burned through him. He tried to keep it quiet, convincing himself the answer wasn't important. But something deep inside wouldn't let him. Words tumbled from his mouth, "Why did you tell me?"

Shifting in his lap, she brought them face-to-face. He could feel the delicate tickle of her breath across his lips. They responded, opening instinctively in preparation to accept whatever she wanted to give him.

Her warm palms rested against the line of his jaw, holding him in place.

"Because you understand. You've suffered. Not just losing your brother, but watching friends and fellow soldiers give their lives." Her fingers slipped across the ink tattooed on his right arm, tracing the dark lines and burst of flames.

He'd gotten it to memorialize a buddy he'd lost in battle. The picture was as close as he could get to the memory of dragging that broken body away from danger as the world continued to explode around them.

He'd never told Quinn anything about it, but apparently he didn't have to for her to know.

"You've seen devastation and poverty and repression. You've felt the twist of those things deep inside and fought them. You *understand*."

He couldn't breathe. His chest burned. But he couldn't tear his gaze away from hers. From the connection creeping out to bridge the distance he'd purposely tried to put between them.

All he could give her was a nod, a single jerky movement. But that seemed to satisfy her.

She'd given him something special. Something she hadn't shared with Michael.

What kind of asshole was he that it mattered…a lot?

7

It HAD BEEN a long time since she'd had to relive the night her parents died. At first, the nightmares had plagued her constantly. The more time that passed—and the more she dealt with the guilt, anger and fear that followed—the less she dreamed. It had been years.

And she had no idea why the full extent of what she'd gone through had spilled out of her mouth to Jace. No, that wasn't entirely right.

What she'd told him was the truth. Michael would have been sympathetic, but he wouldn't have been able to truly grasp what she'd been through and how terribly scary that emotional tailspin had been. How scary it could still be when she didn't quite succeed in clamping down on her responses.

Jace did. He'd lived through his own tailspin. And she knew he was still trying to pull out of it, no matter what he said.

She wanted to help him. Needed to help him. And not simply because it was what she'd been trained for.

She didn't want to see him isolated, closing himself off from everything and everyone.

She could help him. But only if he let her. And so far, every attempt she'd made had been rebuffed....

Jace shifted. He moved her off his lap, putting space she didn't want between them.

The ghost of her nightmare reared up, covering her skin in a clammy film.

He was going to leave her. She didn't want to be alone. Not tonight.

"Wait." A hand on his arm, she stilled him before he could push up and off the bed.

A single eyebrow quirked, he gazed down at her. "Stay."

His eyes went wide, disbelief and something akin to torment flashed across his face before he hid it.

"I don't think that's a good idea, Quinn."

"I don't want to be alone, Jace. I promise I'll behave." She flashed him a smile that hopefully looked innocent. "Trust me, I'm not likely to kiss you again."

Not after the way he'd run from her like she was the devil incarnate. She had a one-humiliating-moment-a-week limit, and it had already been hit.

Dropping the teasing lilt, she let her true vulnerability shine through. "Please. With everything that's been going on...I'm afraid if I'm alone the nightmare will come back."

"And you think me being here will keep it away?"

She lifted her shoulders. "Maybe." She really had no idea, but it sounded like a good enough excuse.

With a sigh that seemed to drag from the very depths of his body, Jace twisted back to the center of the bed. He slithered down the headboard and reached to the floor to gather up the pillows her flailing had knocked to the ground.

Placing one behind her, he waited until she settled back down before taking a pillow for himself and covering them both with the quilt.

There was a gulf of space between them, but that didn't stop his heat from filling the emptiness around her. He wasn't touching her, but she could still feel him. Hear his even breathing and pull the heavy weight of his scent deep into her lungs.

The last dregs of tension that had invaded her body slowly seeped away. Exhaustion claimed her, along with a clear, restful sleep that—considering everything going on—she hadn't expected and was a true gift.

JACE WAS NORMALLY a light sleeper. Years of grabbing snatches here and there in the middle of chaos and danger had taught him the art of resting with one eye open. So it was a shock to awaken and realize he'd been dead to the world.

And that he wasn't alone.

The tentative fingers of dawn crept across the room, invading the darkness that had wrapped around them last night. He couldn't help but watch the gray, gold and pink as it suffused Quinn's skin.

She was still asleep, which made staring at her okay. He was the only one who would ever know.

God, having her here, in his bed, was a fantasy turned reality turned torture, but he allowed himself the luxury of wallowing in it, if just for a few minutes.

His body hummed with the constant, low vibration that assaulted him whenever Quinn was close. He was so used to it, it was normally easy to ignore.

She was gorgeous, her skin flushed with sleep. Her face was relaxed and those lush, tempting lips open just enough to give him a hint of what he couldn't have. The memory of kissing her hit him full force. Hell, he could even taste her.

His body reacted, going from revved to ready in the space of a single heartbeat. His cock throbbed relentlessly, a painful reminder of just how close he was skating to the edge of reason.

Time to get up.

Jace shifted, rolling onto his hip, but he didn't get far. From behind him, Quinn's leg dropped across his thighs. Her foot wiggled between his knees, tangling them together.

He froze. He could have pushed her off, she was tiny enough. But his muscles wouldn't obey.

Behind him, she burrowed deeper, her entire body sliding sinuously against him. Her arm crept up over his hip to settle in the center of his chest.

A low, sleepy sound of satisfaction vibrated against his back. She rocked, her hips pulsing even as her arm and leg tightened to pull him back harder against her.

His honor only went so far....

Surging up and over her, Jace had Quinn on her back beneath him before either of them could think. A startled squeak burst through her parted lips.

"I only have so much strength, Quinn. You can't touch me like that and not expect me to respond."

She blinked up at him through those big brown eyes, heavy with sleep and a languid heat that had him clenching down on an answering surge of need.

The teasing tip of her little pink tongue slipped out to run across her plush lips. Jace groaned deep in the back of his throat.

"Maybe I want you to respond."

He drew in a sharp breath, his lungs filling with the pure essence of her. She wasn't lying. He could feel the radiating heat of her desire slipping off her body.

He wanted to taste her skin. Her mouth.

And he didn't have any more fight left in him.

With a soft curse, he bent to claim her lips. He left her enough space to find some sanity and push him away, but she opened for him. Accepted him. Took him in and gave him everything.

The kiss was explosive, all they'd been holding back smoldering to ashes between them.

Jace's arms began to tremble from the strain of holding himself away from her. Something he'd been doing for years. As if sensing how tight he was still trying to hold on, Quinn arched up, closing the gap between them.

If he wouldn't come to her, she was coming for him.

Wrapping one leg high around his hips, she dug her heel into his rear and drove him down. His body collapsed, half on and half off of her. He expected her to groan beneath his weight. Instead, the most amazing sound fell from her parted lips—a sigh of relief.

He felt the echo of it straight through to his bones. He drank the sound in, taking it, cherishing it.

She wanted him. At least for this one moment.

Comfort, relief, a mad physical need…he didn't care. Whatever had driven her into his arms, Jace was going to take it. He wasn't strong enough for anything else. Not where Quinn was concerned.

The covers tangled between them. His desperate hands searched for her anyway, fighting the folds of material blocking her from him.

With a breathless laugh, Quinn sat up, pushing

against his shoulders. For the briefest moment, panic suffused him, and he was afraid that just as he'd decided to give in she'd decided to call a halt.

He shouldn't have worried.

Climbing up to her knees, Quinn sent the quilt to the floor, clearing the way between them.

The T-shirt she was wearing was so big it hung off one shoulder, leaving her bare. The hem was crooked, slashing from barely below one hip to several inches down the other thigh. Her skin was creamy pale and he wanted to spend hours just licking it, worshipping every single freckle dotting her.

Jace watched her, drinking in each minute detail. The laughter died on her lips, fading from her big, beautiful eyes to be replaced with a heat that nearly singed him.

Crossing her arms, she reached for the bottom of the shirt and pulled it over her head.

God, she was gorgeous, inside and out. So luminous.

He reached for her, his wide palms spanning her hips. Hell, he could practically reach from the curve of her breast to the edge of her hipbone. She made him feel…big and graceless. She was so tiny and delicate. Precious.

Rolling to his back, he tugged until she fell against him. His mouth found her skin, licking along the ridge of her collarbone. He felt her shiver, saw the wave of goose bumps that scattered over her. She arched into his caress. Her fingers curled into him where they'd landed on his chest.

He took his time, savoring the salty tang of her skin filling his mouth. His hands swept up and down the curve of her back, each time dipping further and further beneath the waistband of her panties until his palms cupped the high, round globes of her ass.

She was shivering, the slight tremble racking her entire body.

"God, Jace, you're killing me," she groaned when his exploration got close to the tight pink tip of one breast, but didn't touch.

"I've thought about this for a very long time, Quinn. I will not be rushed. Before we're done, my mouth will be on every single one of your freckles."

She whimpered, a cross between anticipation and torture.

But Quinn Keller had never been the kind of woman to sit still and wait for anything. Especially something she wanted.

He loved that about her.

Throwing a leg over his hip, she straddled him, bringing them tight together. Even through the layers between them, he could feel the blazing heat of her sex. Reaching down, she shifted her panties out of the way, settling right over him.

A red-hot haze blocked out everything but the feel of her.

"Aw, hell," he breathed.

THIS WAS NOT what she'd planned when she'd woken up. But Quinn wasn't going to quibble. Not when she finally had Jace where she'd wanted him for so long.

At first, she'd thought she was in the middle of another dream. Until she'd followed her instincts, wrapped her leg and arm around him and felt real muscle and bone.

By then it was too late to take it back. She was

draped around him like a sweater…and it had felt too good to run her hands along the planes of his body. The silky-smooth texture of him, roughened by the dusting of hair across his chest.

And now…she was straddling his hips, driving them both crazy by rubbing them together. Spark to tinder.

Quinn sucked in a breath when his large hands wrapped around her waist. He surged up and rolled her beneath him. Somewhere in the maneuver, her panties slid down her thighs. And his mouth finally found her breast, tugging the tight, aching tip into the deep recesses of his mouth.

She cried out, unable to keep the sound of pleasure in. It was as if a direct line ran straight from the rasp of his tongue to her throbbing sex.

Was it possible to come from just that? Maybe, considering she'd been fantasizing about this for a while… and hadn't been touched for just as long.

Her fingers were buried deep in the hair at his nape, holding him in place, silently begging for more.

She was so preoccupied she didn't brace for the jolt of feeling his hand slip up the inside of her thigh. Parting her. Diving inside.

Her hips bucked. Her mouth dropped open on a keening cry that he swallowed.

God, she wanted more. Needed more. All of him.

"Jace," she whispered, the sound harsh with urgency.

She couldn't stay still, not with his fingers slipping and sliding through her sex. Pumping in and out. Thumbing her clit. Driving her crazy, but not giving her enough.

Never enough.

Frantic, she reached for him. Running her palms

across the peaks and valleys of his hard, honed body. Maybe his long hours of training were worth it. As long as he wanted to use *her* for relief instead of that damn cage.

She tunneled beneath the waistband of his boxers, finally finding what she wanted.

She'd felt him nestled against her, when he'd tackled her to the ground.

But there was nothing like filling her hands with him. Touching, testing. Sliding up and down his hard length.

Squeezing, she relished the deep rumble of his groan and the way he watched her from beneath half-closed lids. Those clear blue eyes glittered, heat, need and promise sending another tremor through her body.

Pleasure. She wanted to give it to him. Give him anything that would banish the shadows that haunted the edges of his eyes. Make him forget, if only for a few moments.

Curling up, she flicked her tongue out, taking her first, full lap at him.

His taste exploded across her tongue, potent and salty. Honeyed heat. God, she wanted more. Everything he'd give her.

Widening her mouth, Quinn took him in. Her eyelids slid shut as sensations bombarded her—the stutter of his groan trailing off into a jagged rasp.

The fever of his silky skin. The wave of response sweeping through her own body, making her tingle and clench and burn.

Up and down, she moved. Sucking hard and soft. Fast and slow. Lapping, laving, loving. Quinn wanted to stay here with him forever, giving pleasure, letting this drive her higher.

She should have known Jace wouldn't be satisfied with that. He wasn't the kind of man who took. He gave. More than he had. More than he should. In everything he did.

His hands wrapped around the back of her head, burying in her hair, letting strands twine around his fingers. With the leverage, he gently, relentlessly pulled her away.

A whimper of protest rippled through her throat. She felt like a child who'd just lost her favorite toy.

She wanted to finish what she'd started. But the moment her gaze collided with his all thought fled, right along with her powers of speech.

Jace Hyland was intense. She didn't need anyone to tell her that. She'd known it the first moment they'd met. Could read it in the set line of his jaw, muscles stone hard across his shoulders and back.

A few months after she and Michael had started seeing each other, Michael had taken her home for Sunday dinner. Like everything else, they'd talked about it at length before she met his family. That was Michael—purposeful, attentive and cautious.

She'd liked the steady easiness of him. Of their relationship. Of who she could be when they were together.

He'd told her about his older brother. Nothing that had prepared her for the impact of Jace. It didn't matter that she was already in love with Michael. Even then, her body had responded to him.

To his simmering power, the silent, intense way he'd watched her all evening, as if she was taking the most important test of her life and he alone would determine if she passed or failed.

Nervous energy had run through her body. She'd never experienced anything like it. Constant awareness. It was exhausting and exhilarating at the same time.

She had to admit that, on that first night, she'd been so happy to leave. To get away from Jace and back to the comfort and contentment of the life she was building with Michael.

She'd already had plenty of drama in her short life and didn't need any more.

Jace was combustible energy and barely leashed control.

The way his blue eyes glittered at her now reminded her of that first night. His entire focus was on her. She could almost believe that in this single moment nothing else existed for him outside of *her*.

It was powerful and provocative. Being the sole focus of a man like Jace could definitely become addictive.

Quinn's stomach rolled with badly timed trepidation. There was no going back from this. They wouldn't be able to laugh it off or pretend.

But even as the fear coiled tight, she couldn't make herself stop. Courage was reaching out and taking what you wanted, even if it scared you senseless.

She'd been safe for too damn long.

He loomed over her, big and sheltering and strong. But he didn't move.

Jace watched her. Saw her. Looked far deeper than anyone probably ever had. There was a part of her that waited for him to decide she wasn't worth it and turn away, leaving her alone all over again.

She'd been alone for so long. She should be used to

it. Was, really. But in that moment, if Jace turned from her it might just crush her, as none of the other trage-dies in her life had. They'd tried, but she was stronger than the grief and misfortune.

A lump formed in the back of her throat and her eyes burned. She wasn't stronger than this. Than him.

Slowly, his thumb brushed across her cheek, gliding along the edge of her cheekbone. Then the roughened pad snagged at the center of her bottom lip, tugging it open.

Longing, apprehension, wonder and a tinge of guilt all twisted inside her. It was too much. Her chest ached with the pressure of it all. She needed the pleasure she knew he could make her feel.

Rearing up, she claimed his mouth, diving inside to tangle her tongue with his. She reveled in the scrape of him across her sensitive taste buds and the jolt of en-ergy that went straight through her.

Jace groaned, low and deep. And suddenly she got her wish.

Gone was the controlled seduction, the distance he'd still been holding between them. Quinn was flat on her back, stretched beneath him, arms held in place above her head before she could blink.

His mouth found the long column of her throat and sucked. He punctuated the caress with a nipping bite before whispering, "I can't keep my hands off you any-more. I don't have enough control for that. I need you like I haven't needed anything before."

His words stole her breath. They were a seduction all their own. Pleasant warmth spread through her and the only response she could possibly give him was, "Yes. Please, yes."

He reached above her, stretching out so that her mouth aligned with the tempting expanse of his chest. Quinn scraped her tongue across the ridge of muscles there.

She heard the squealing sound of wood against wood. Fumbling. Didn't really care what he was doing, not when she was so engrossed in tasting him.

Not until he dropped back to her, a foil packet held between them like a sacrificial offering to some wicked god. Quinn's mouth curved. Thank heaven he was thinking clearly because until that moment the word *condom* hadn't been anywhere close to her brain.

It had been a hell of a long time since she'd needed to worry about protection and birth control.

"Just so you know, I haven't been with anyone since…" Quinn's voice trailed off. Michael was already a specter between them, and she didn't want to give voice to his name. Not now. Not like this.

The only other person Quinn wanted in this bed right now was Jace.

Strengthening her voice, she continued, "For a couple of years. I'm clean and I have an IUD."

Jace nodded. "I'm clean, tested regularly and always careful."

Snatching the square from between his fingers, Quinn tossed it away. "I want to feel you, just you," she whispered.

Jace didn't say anything. He didn't have to. The way his heated gaze bored into her, consumed her, was enough to tell her he wanted that, too.

Hooking an arm beneath her knee, Jace pressed gently until she opened for him. She expected him to surge inside. Wanted him to put her out of her misery. Once again, he surprised her, taking his time. Torturing her.

She could feel him right there, at the aching entrance to her body. But he didn't take what she was happy to offer.

He rocked against her, pushing in an inch before retreating, giving her a little more each time.

Her hands tightened on his shoulders, trying to urge him to give her what she wanted. But he wouldn't be rushed.

"Jace, you're killing me," she whispered.

Reaching down, he trailed his lips along her temple, across her eyelids and along her jaw. "Shh, beautiful. I'm going to savor every last moment, in case this is all I'll ever get."

His words sent her world spinning. They were tinged with torment and a reverence that surprised and thrilled her.

No man had ever said anything like that to her. Something so sensual. Something that made her feel cherished and...*needed.*

Her fingers bracketed his jaws as she pulled his face closer to hers. From somewhere deep inside, a confession she never meant to make spilled from her lips. "Jace, I don't want this to be all we get. Not when I've wanted you for so long."

All the breath exploded from his body. The force of it burst across her skin. And then his hot mouth was on hers, devouring and demanding, and yet somehow soothing.

Or maybe that was just the relief of not having to fight herself anymore.

Before she could get her bearings again, Jace finally

gave her what she'd wanted all along. Surging deep, he filled her completely.

Quinn couldn't stop the bone-deep groan of contentment that roared up from her belly. The sound morphed to a whimper when he undulated his hips as he pulsed in and out. He did it over and over again until her skin was slick with sweat, her muscles quivered with the pressure of being held just on the edge of oblivion and pleasure swamped her in waves that threatened to take her under and never let her back up again.

Her fingers dug into his skin, trying to hold on to the only solid thing left in her world—him. She could feel the release building, just out of reach, like a wave rolling toward shore, gathering strength and height with each yard traveled.

God, it was going to be too much. Leave her open and vulnerable. But it was too late to stop, not that she would even if she could.

And she wasn't wrong. When it hit, her release took away everything, leaving only the pleasure he'd given her, the way he cradled her body and the soft murmur of his incoherent words in her ear. Contentment and happiness radiated out from where they joined.

But he didn't stop. Jace demanded more than she thought possible. Relentlessly, he drove them both higher. Caresses, kisses, words trailed across her over-sensitized skin. He tempted and coaxed, knowing just how to touch her to draw the moment out.

The crest of the first release had barely subsided when another was building. And he was right with her. Her hands slipped across his sweat-slicked skin. She licked at any piece of him she could get, savoring the taste of him on her tongue, the sounds, her cries mixing with his groans.

And the entire time, Jace held her gaze, refusing to let her go. The connection was almost too much, and yet she couldn't break it. Couldn't look away from what he was giving her—a glimpse into a part of himself he rarely shared.

With each passing moment his body cranked tighter. His building tension increased her own as they climbed together. Reaching between them, Jace found the tight bundle of nerves begging for his touch and rubbed. It was all she needed, her keening cry reverberating around them.

Jace groaned, his eyes closing, as he finally let himself go. His jaw clamped tight, holding in the sounds she was desperate to hear. She wanted it, wanted the proof of his pleasure ringing through her ears. But she could feel the kick as he exploded deep inside.

Wrapping her arms around his strong shoulders, Quinn held on tight. Her heels dug into the backs of his thighs, urging him closer. His ragged, uneven breaths burst against her damp skin, sending shivers through her already overloaded body.

After several minutes, Jace shifted, putting space between them. Quinn forced back the urge to tighten her hold and keep him close. She wasn't ready for the fantasy to end.

But that one simple motion pulled the decision from her hands because reality crowded in anyway.

They'd just had sex. Now what was she going to do?

Looming over her, Jace stared down at her, piercing her with those damn blue eyes that saw way too much and gave nothing away.

Anxiety and uncertainty flipped through her exhausted system. His next words did nothing to dispel the reaction.

"Just how long have you wanted this?"

8

SHE TRIED TO squirm away, but Jace wouldn't let her. Not even when she looked at him with such open vulnerability.

It went far beyond what she'd just given him physically. He'd always known Quinn would be an amazing lover. She was the kind of person who gave everything, spent her life taking care of other people, and would do the same for anyone she let into her bed.

She had so much love to give, which was one reason he'd been trying for months to convince her to find someone new. If anyone in this world deserved to be happy, it was Quinn.

He could see she didn't want to talk about the words she'd accidentally let free in the heat of a passionate moment. Tough.

Jace used his leverage to keep her pinned beneath him and asked again, "How long have you wanted this?"

She tried to turn her face away, but he needed the window into her thoughts. Cupping her chin, he applied gentle pressure until she didn't have a choice but to look at him.

His chest tightened when he saw the sheen of tears she was fighting. He almost caved, but that's when she finally answered.

"How long have I been physically attracted to you? From the very first time we met."

Heat suffused her skin and disgust clouded her eyes. It cut straight through him. He didn't want her to regret what they'd just done, because he sure as hell didn't.

But how could she not? They'd both been overwhelmed by physical attraction. Sure, his feelings for her went much deeper, but her feelings for him probably didn't. And now she was struggling with the guilt over what they'd done.

Something he could understand, because he'd been fighting the same thing for so long—wanting her and knowing it was so, so wrong.

He wanted to rail against fate. Why couldn't he have met Quinn first? Why was the perfect woman put in front of him and then made completely unavailable?

And then he'd been given a taste only to have reality shoved in his face.

Fury mixed with impatience and frustration. He didn't know how to handle this.

But what he did know was that he wouldn't let Quinn beat herself up over moving on. Maybe that was what he was supposed to give her—the first step toward a new life.

And if that's what she needed from him...

"Don't," Jace growled, his fingers tightening their hold. "Don't you dare feel guilty, Quinn. You didn't do a damn thing wrong. *We* didn't do anything wrong."

"Then why does it feel like it?" she whispered, looking up at him through eyes awash with unshed tears.

"This isn't just about tonight. I was attracted to you, Jace, long before Michael was gone. Being in the same room…it was always difficult. No matter how hard I tried not to, I always found myself watching you. The way you move, all power and grace, was just…too much."

Her words rocked him. They were so unexpected. "I had no idea," he breathed out.

"Good," she whispered. "Then maybe Michael didn't, either."

Anguish clouded her eyes and she jerked her gaze away. Jace trailed a soothing finger along the ridge of her cheek.

"You loved him, Quinn."

It wasn't a question. He'd always known it was the truth. Wanted that for his brother. For her.

"Yes."

This time instead of forcing her to meet his gaze, he chased hers, refusing to let her hide—from him or this.

"You didn't love me."

Her caramel eyes widened. "No, of course not."

"Quinn, you didn't do anything wrong. What you felt for me—feel for me—is just chemistry. It's physical. What you had with Michael was so much more. He knew that."

She shook her head, strands of her dark hair slipping across creamy pale skin.

"You didn't act on what you were feeling. Hell, you didn't do a single thing to indicate it was even a possibility. You. Did. Nothing. Wrong."

A soft voice whispered through his head that he hadn't, either. But the voice was mistaken.

While Quinn had finally given in to her body's natural needs, taking what was available, he had been lusting after her for years.

And not just her body.

He'd wanted what Michael had—her smiles, mornings in her arms, and even her emotional outbursts. He'd wanted to hold her and tease her and fight with her.

He'd wanted more than he should, and he still did.

But for the moment he was willing to take whatever she wanted to give him. And at the same time he'd help her heal so she could move on—from them both.

Instead of making the guilt fade as he'd hoped, his words had the gold flecks in her eyes flashing. "I'm here now."

"And Michael is dead."

His words might have been harsh, but they were true. And apparently she needed the reminder.

Michael was gone and he wasn't coming back. "He wouldn't want you to spend your life mourning him, Quinn. Hell, I heard him say that exact thing to you the last night in the hospital. He wanted you to be happy."

"I am happy," she said, her words full of defiance neither of them believed.

"No, you're not. Not really."

Her sharp intake of breath surprised him. "You don't know what you're talking about."

His smile was grim. "Oh, but I do. You forget, I've listened to stories about your life for the past two years. You don't see the friends you and Michael had before. You barely speak to your sister. You don't even have a pet. Your life consists of work, work and more work. And while what you do is admirable, it isn't enough."

The fire in her eyes flashed hotter. Her mouth thinned and her hands found his chest, pushing against him. But he didn't budge. He wasn't going to let her ignore what he was saying. Not anymore.

Gentling his words, he narrowed the space between them, staring hard into her eyes and hoping she'd really listen to what he said. "You can't use your work to hide from your own life, Quinn, not anymore."

"I'm not—" she began hotly, but he cut her off.

"You are. Solving everyone else's problems while you keep yourself locked inside a sterile, safe little world."

A choking sound erupted from her throat. At first, he thought it was temper. Until the tears she'd been holding at bay began to slip down her cheeks.

"I don't…" she said, tears clogging the words. "I don't know how to stop. It hurts so bad, losing someone. I've done it so many times. Too many. I don't think I can do it again, let myself care about someone and have them taken away."

God, he wanted to comfort her. Take her pain and just make it disappear. But that wasn't possible.

At least he could hold her, give her a safe, soft place to let it all out.

His mouth buried against her temple, he murmured, "Let me help you."

"How?"

Curling down to her, he took her mouth. This kiss was different, soft and sweet, easy and comfortable. "With this."

Continuing to see her, touch her, love her, was probably the stupidest thing he would ever do. Although it wasn't as if he had the strength to walk away from her—not now.

"We're stuck together, Quinn, at least until this thing

with Warren blows over. Neither of us seems capable of ignoring the physical attraction burning between us. Why should we try? We're not doing anything wrong. And maybe when this is over you'll be better prepared to let someone else into your life."

He'd be the bridge between Michael and the rest of her tomorrows.

God, it was going to hurt when it was over.

He already loved her. Falling *in love* with her was inevitable.

But for the moment, he'd take what he could get and worry about the aftermath later. He had plenty of experience living with pain, guilt and regret.

Pulling back, Jace smoothed his fingers over her face. "Just so there's no confusion, you weren't the only one struggling with inappropriate thoughts. I've wanted you from that first moment, too. It was hell trying to keep my hands off you, even before Michael got sick."

That struggle was one of the reasons he'd agreed so easily to give Michael a kidney, even though it cost him the career he loved and needed.

Not that he wouldn't have made the decision anyway, he would have. But the niggling guilt had spurred him to give his brother whatever he needed no matter the personal price.

Because Michael deserved a long and happy life with a girl like Quinn. And Quinn deserved the easy, comfortable, content life she would have had with his brother.

All Jace had to offer was a restless need that bubbled up inside him no matter how hard he fought against it. He was remote and difficult. He'd seen too much in the world to believe in things that were warm and fuzzy, not that he ever had.

Instead of seeing the twisted, black mess of a soul he tried so hard to hide—and running, the way she probably should—Quinn moved closer. She reached for him, mirroring his hold on her face, running the soft pad of her finger across his temple and down his cheek.

"Is that why you can't let him go? Because you feel guilty—not that he died, but that you wanted me?"

She saw way too much. And he was afraid eventually she was going to see it all—and realize she could do so much better than a broken, useless soldier.

"No." The word cracked so he tried again, but something different came out, a confession he hadn't intended to make. "Yes."

Her arms wrapped around him tight and squeezed. Her cheek found his chest and rubbed. "Oh, Jace. You didn't do anything wrong, either."

"Yes, I did. What if I'd refused? If I hadn't been driven by guilt and had taken the selfish way out? If he'd gotten a kidney from someone else maybe he'd still be alive."

He couldn't look at her, see the horror and pity that he knew must be filling her, because it utterly swamped him.

Silence stretched between them, reinforcing the recriminations he'd been nursing deep inside for two long years.

"You know that's not true, Jace," she finally whispered. "It wasn't your fault. The doctors even said your kidney was perfect. It was just one of those things—not every transplant is successful."

God, he wanted to believe her, but he couldn't shake the sensation that when Michael had needed him most, he'd failed.

* * *

His words were still ringing in Quinn's ears hours later when Jace dragged her to his gym for a quick self-defense lesson. The memory of his expression—so devastated and broken—when he'd claimed Michael's death was his fault tore her apart a little more each time she replayed their conversation.

She wanted to fix it. Fix him. But there was nothing she could do or say. She'd tried. Not just this morning, but for the past two years, and he wasn't listening.

Which only broke her heart that much more.

She'd dealt with difficult cases over the years. It was usually the teenagers who got to her. She always wanted to break through their protective layers so they'd let her help. Maybe because that was the age she'd been when she'd struggled and needed someone to force through all the grief and confusion and pain.

It was easy for her to identify with them, even if they were all fighting different demons.

With Jace, she was at a loss. If one of her colleagues had come to her with the same situation, she knew exactly what she'd have said—they were too close to help. But her heart told her she couldn't walk away from his pain.

Unfortunately, she wasn't going to solve the problem in a day, even if her body was full of restless energy, a constant buzzing that told her she should be doing *something*.

Although the something she had in mind would hardly have looked like this.

"Concentrate, Quinn."

She frowned, looking over at Jace. "I don't want to do this."

"Duly noted."

"And ignored."

Jace sighed, tilting his head back so he could stare up at the dirty metal ceiling above them. It was almost painful to follow his gaze and take in the decrepit structure he'd brought her to. Especially when she knew he was entreating the heavens for strength in dealing with her.

If he wasn't careful, not even a deity would be able to protect him from her temper. She was holding on to it by a thin strand as it was.

"We've already been over this. After last night, you need to know how to protect yourself."

Which was how she found herself standing in the middle of what had once been an industrial building but was now functioning as a gym. The kind with concrete floors and metal cages and torn punching bags held together by duct tape.

Several paces away men were pounding on the bags, the grunts of their efforts exploding into the room. The links of rusty metal chains clanked together in a repeated rhythm that tore at her nerves.

After the spectacle of Jace's fight, she really didn't want to be here. However, she did see the wisdom in what he was saying. And the thought of being able to defend herself if—when—Warren showed up again did hold merit.

"Fine." She sighed.

Jace just grinned at her. Snagging her hand, he directed her to a corner of the room where several thick foam mats had been laid out across the floor.

Positioning her in the center, he walked around behind her.

"Okay, I'm going to come at you. Try to deflect my attack."

She could feel him. Hear him. The soft, even cadence of his breath. The dark, sinful scent of him wafting out to envelope her.

She was distracted, unprepared when his arms wrapped around her chest, pinning her arms to her sides and pulling her back against his chest. Her feet left the floor.

Her first instinct was to melt. Even after only one night with him, her body had taken over from her brain.

Until his soft voice whispered into her ear. "Think, Quinn. How are you going to get out of this? What leverage do you have?"

Her arms were useless. But her feet dangled right at the perfect height to smash into his shins. Using every ounce of power, she attempted to kick his leg.

Jace easily blocked her movements, stepping forward and tangling her leg between his own, taking her momentum away and making her heels useless.

Frustration bubbled inside her until he rumbled, "Good. What else?" into her ear.

Her ear. Her head. She was perfectly positioned to slam the back of it into his face. Even as the thought flitted across her brain, she hesitated.

She didn't want to hurt him.

As if sensing her thoughts, Jace's hold on her tightened. It didn't hurt, but left her feeling trapped. Helpless. Memories from Warren's visit the night before flooded her with fear and uncertainty.

She'd grabbed that knife as if she knew what to do with it, but she didn't have a clue. Sure, she could have drawn blood, but it probably wouldn't have been enough to stop him.

And even if he'd come at her, she wasn't sure she'd have been able to hurt him with it. Her stomach turned at the thought of wounding another person or at the realization she was probably too weak to defend herself.

Suddenly, Jace's hold on her was too much. She couldn't breathe. "Let me go," she wheezed, even as she began struggling in earnest. Her body squirmed in the limited amount of space she had to maneuver. The single leg that was free flailed. And when she finally worked an arm free, she used it to slam repeatedly into the hands holding her.

But he didn't let her go.

Instead, his calm, steady voice floated into her ear. "Use your elbow, it's one of the hardest points on your body. And the back of your head. Find the softest, most vulnerable places you can and attack. Over and over again until you get free."

"I can't," she panted. "I don't want to hurt you."

His chuckle finally broke through the sheen of panic that had been muffling her reaction. It pissed her off.

"You can't hurt me, sweetheart. I know exactly what I'm doing."

Okay, he'd asked for it.

Flashing out with her elbow, she forced it into his soft—although that was definitely a relative term considering the hard muscle that covered every inch of him—middle. Without waiting for a response, she reared forward before slamming her head against his chin.

Jace let out a wheezing groan, collapsing toward her. His already folding body probably protected him from the full impact of her skull. His arms loosened around her, finally letting her free.

But her relief was short-lived when he fell to his knees on the mat beside her before keeling onto his side. One arm wrapped around his middle, he rolled onto his back. His eyes screwed shut in pain.

Quinn dropped to his side, her knees smarting when they hit the mat.

"Jace. Oh, my God, are you okay?"

He let out a tortured sound that had her heart thumping erratically in her throat. He was clutching his side, the one with his good kidney. She hadn't thought about that when she'd jabbed.

What had she done?

Scrambling for his shirt, she tried to lift it out of the way so she could see, although she really had no idea what she was looking for.

He'd taken several body shots the other night during the fight. It had been easy to forget when he'd been acting as if he was totally fine, but maybe he had been badly injured and she'd made it worse.

One moment she was kneeling beside him, the next her back hit the dark blue mat and all the air whooshed out of her lungs.

The world spun, not just from her change in position, but from the sudden loss of oxygen.

But it only took her a few seconds to recover. And when she did it was to look up into Jace's wide, mischievous grin.

"Never, ever, trust your attacker. Or stop to make sure they're okay. Once you get free, run."

His body pinned hers to the floor. The heavy weight of his thigh pressed against her hip. The hard wall of his chest loomed above her. The muscles in his arms bulged on either side of her head.

She wanted to twist her head and bite him. And then lick him.

Suddenly, the temperature in the room changed. Or maybe the heat was coming from her own body.

Her gaze snagged on his mouth. She wanted it on hers, wanted to feel his lips nibbling her skin.

Jace groaned, only this time it had nothing to do with pain.

"Don't look at me that way."

"What way?" she asked, her voice breathy.

"Like you want to devour me."

"Maybe I do."

His arms began to tremble. She relished the quiver, visual confirmation of his reaction to her.

"Not here," he growled.

Shifting beneath him, Quinn wrapped her arms around his neck and used the leverage to pull herself flush with him. Finding his mouth, she teased, "Why not?"

"Because there are too many eyes."

Distracting him with a full-blown kiss, she wrapped her legs high around his thighs and then surged against him. Jace dropped back to the mat, letting her roll on top of him.

She kept them connected through the entire move, unwilling to give up the delicious taste of him on her tongue. Her hands roamed across his chest and down his hips. Drawing her knees up his thighs, she straddled him and then finally pushed away.

Sitting astride him, she delighted in the way he

looked up at her, dumbfounded, his icy-blue eyes a little glazed.

From across the room someone whistled. She ignored them, instead putting her entire focus into Jace beneath her.

He felt so strong and solid, covered with ropy muscles. But he wasn't, because he had a weakness that not even his strength could guard.

"Did I really hurt you?"

"No," he answered slowly. Too slowly.

"Jace," she said in a warning tone.

"I'm still a little sore from Friday."

"Then why the hell did you ask me to hit you?"

Shifting beneath her, Jace moved her backward until she was perched on the hard ridge of his thighs. He rose, wrapping his arms around her waist and back to keep her snug in place.

They sat there on the floor. Jace watched her, his gaze intense as always. But there was something more. This close, she couldn't miss the subtle emotions playing across his features.

Possessiveness, need and something softer.

"Because there was no way I was letting anyone else put his arms around you."

Threading her hands into his hair, Quinn tugged at the strands. "Silly, frustrating, incorrigible man. What am I going to do with you?"

"Take me to dinner? Mom and Dad asked me to bring you by when they found out what's been going on."

Panic filled her. She wasn't ready for that. Hell, she didn't know what she and Jace were doing yet. How was she supposed to act in front of his parents? Michael's parents.

They'd always loved her. And she loved them.

Scrambling off Jace's lap, Quinn found her feet. Her gaze darted around the cavernous room, but there was nowhere to go.

"Hey, relax," Jace said, wrapping his arms around her and pulling her back into his chest.

She couldn't push away from the comfort he offered, not when she was so full of turmoil.

Burying her nose in his chest, she asked, "What are we going to tell them?"

She felt his body stiffen as he finally realized what had spooked her. Part of her regretted the words, but as she opened her mouth to take them back, he relaxed again.

"Nothing. Quinn, this is none of their business. They're worried about you and just wanted to see you. We'll go have dinner, just like we've done a thousand times before. Everything will be fine."

She hoped he was right, but even as they left the gym, heading back to his place so they could clean up and change, Quinn wasn't so certain.

9

His mother didn't bother saying hi. Practically before the echo of the doorbell had rung through the house, she had the door jerked open and Quinn wrapped tight in her arms.

"We're so glad you're okay," his mom said.

Quinn threw him a startled look before wrapping her arms around his mom and joining in the hug.

"I'm fine, Naomi. It's nothing."

Pulling back, his mom gave them both a scowl before ushering them into the house. As always, she was a whirlwind of activity. Taking coats, motioning them to the sofa even as she scolded.

"It isn't nothing. Jace told us this man is a real threat. What I want to know is why we had to hear about it from him."

A guilty blush crept up Quinn's cheeks, but she kept her gaze steady as she responded, "Because I didn't want to worry you."

His mom made a harrumphing noise before heading to the open archway leading through to the kitchen. As soon as her back was turned, Quinn threw Jace a scowl of her own. No doubt they'd be discussing her displeasure later.

Not that he really cared.

His parents loved Quinn. His mom, especially, worried about her whether there was a physical threat or not. They considered her their daughter and he knew the hurt that his mom was trying to hide was very real. It bothered her that Quinn didn't turn to them for help when she needed it.

Although, he didn't think Quinn turned to anyone for help, so his mother really shouldn't take it personally.

From the back of the house, his dad appeared, wiping his hands on a towel. No doubt his mom had pulled him out from beneath the car engine he'd been working on in the garage so he could wash up before they arrived.

He clapped Jace across the shoulders and leaned down to kiss Quinn's upturned cheek. "Hi, Sam."

"Beautiful as always, Quinn. Hope you're hungry. Naomi's been fussing in the kitchen all day preparing your favorites."

Of course she had been. His mom was quintessentially Southern and felt there was no better demonstration of love than copious amounts of food.

"Y'all get your drinks," his mom called from the kitchen.

The heavenly scent of pot roast, mashed potatoes, corn pudding and yeast rolls filled the room. The warmth of the oven hung over them, making the air feel damp and close.

The table was small, just a four-seater. It was all that would fit in the space and all they'd needed growing up. Unfortunately, it also meant that when he sat, his knee bumped into Quinn's thigh, sending a thrill of awareness jolting up his spine.

From her quick inhale she'd felt the same thing, which didn't do much to help his frame of mind.

Jerking his attention to his mom, he caught her narrowed, shrewd eyes watching him. Suddenly, he felt like a wayward teenager trying to get away with lying to his mother. Something he'd never managed. And not because he was a terrible liar.

She'd just been that tuned in to the domain she ruled with a soft smile and an iron fist.

Quinn's freak-out over coming tonight hadn't been great for his ego. Not that he necessarily wanted to confess to his mama that he'd slept with Quinn, at least not yet. But the fact that she'd practically come unglued at the idea of his parents finding out...

It had hurt, even as his brain told him it shouldn't.

He'd wanted her for so long, it was hard not to want to crow like a rooster and tell the entire world now, even if he knew it wouldn't last.

Quinn was right to be wary. He needed to get control of himself and his reactions before his observant mother put the pieces together and realized what he'd done.

So they sat through dinner, making small talk about their lives. Jace told his parents he'd taken leave, but let them think it was to watch over Quinn instead of prepare for his fight. His mom already had enough to worry about. The fight was over and he was fine.

Besides, he didn't feel up to a scolding.

Together, they explained the situation with Warren and he assured everyone—including Quinn—that he had her covered and nothing was going to happen.

After dessert, his dad stood up from the table, rested a hand across his shoulder and said, "Come out to the garage. Let me show you what I've been working on."

There was a part of him reluctant to leave Quinn in the house, even knowing that she'd be perfectly safe.

Looking at her, he quirked an eyebrow in silent question. If she wanted him to stay, he'd find a way to refuse. Or sweep her along with them.

But the small smile she gave him silently told him she'd be fine.

With a few simple gestures and less than thirty seconds, they'd had a full conversation. It was something he'd seen her do with Michael. Something he'd envied, the ease of their connection.

A band tightened across his chest, squeezing painfully as he pushed up from the table and followed his dad outside.

The garage was a separate building at the back of the half-acre lot behind the house. There were two bay doors and a short drive leading up from the alley that ran behind the tidy row of houses.

Sometime before his parents had bought the house thirty years earlier, the previous owners had added a single car garage to the side of the house and a drive leading up to it from the road. That was where his mom parked.

This building had become his father's. And as they'd gotten older, a place for Jace and Michael to come and pretend to be the men they weren't quite yet. When he was home, his father had taken them both out there, teaching them everything he knew about cars.

Some guys, growing up with a father who was more absent than present, might have become jaded or bitter. But not Jace. Or Michael.

Maybe it was because when his father had been home he'd given them his full attention. Spent time with them.

Punished them when they needed it and lectured when he was disappointed in them. It was enough to keep them in line.

Rolling up the door to the first bay, his dad stood back and let him take in the beauty that was the vintage Mustang. The car was the kind of machine no one made anymore. Beautiful lines, sturdy structure and a lightning-fast engine.

Admiring her bright red paint, Jace could imagine finding a deserted country road and letting the engine open wide, wind whipping through his hair and adrenaline pumping into his blood.

"She's amazing, Dad. Looks like you're almost done." This had been his dad's project for the past eighteen months or so. Jace had seen the car many times. He'd also watched his dad slowly transform a piece of junk into a masterpiece several times in his life. But it never got old. "You going to sell this one or keep her?"

Shaking his head, Sam ran a loving hand over the curve of the hood, almost as if he was actually caressing the powerful engine hidden beneath. "Not sure yet," he said, but Jace could hear the reverence and longing lurking in his deep voice.

Oh, he was keeping this one. And Jace was glad. His dad had put hours of blood, sweat and tears into plenty of cars. All of their vehicles were always in top running condition, because his father wouldn't allow his wife and sons to drive something that could fail and leave them stranded and vulnerable while he was several states away with no way to help.

But the man had always insisted on driving an old beat-up car whenever he was home. The thing ran just fine, but was never much to look at. Michael had asked him once, when they were younger, why he never kept any of the cars he rebuilt for himself. His dad had responded that he didn't need anything flashy, especially when the cars he rebuilt and sold for a nice profit could provide safety and comfort for his wife and sons while he was gone.

Those words had stuck with Jace for years.

Turning, Sam let his hips settle against the hood, arms crossed over the massive barrel chest not even age could take from him.

"So, tell me the truth, how much trouble is Quinn in?"

"Enough. Warren's a nasty guy. We filed a report when he broke into her place, but until he does something more there isn't much the cops can do. Especially since the man is connected. He's dangerous."

"I never would have expected it from him. The man has a sterling reputation."

"Sure, he was careful to cultivate that image. According to his wife, his squeaky-clean public persona is an act, and not just with her. Quinn told me about some of her injuries and scars, and it chills me to the bone."

Just talking about it had rage rising in his gut. Part of him hoped Warren would be stupid enough to take another run at Quinn just so Jace would have a reason to beat the shit out of him.

The rest of him hoped the tightening net of protection around her was enough of a deterrent to keep Warren far away.

Unfortunately, his instincts told him that wasn't very likely. Quinn was the quickest way to Caroline.

"Apparently, he's also been using his legitimate businesses and charitable donations as a front to launder money for a crime syndicate up north. Quinn's told as much as she knows to the police already, but it isn't much. They're trying to untangle the money trail, but without help… And Caroline is too scared to testify right now. They're hoping with some time and distance she'll come around. But I don't know how long Quinn is willing to wait for Warren to be locked up. She's already champing at the bit to get back to work and it's just not a great idea."

"That girl always was impetuous." Sam's words might have sounded like disapproval, except for his soft tone. His voice was filled more with exasperation and acceptance than anything else.

"She definitely tends to put everyone else above self-preservation."

"Always has."

They both nodded. His dad's gaze dropped to a spot on the concrete floor. A comfortable silence stretched between them. That was the great thing about his dad, he didn't need to fill the moment. Maybe it was all the time Sam had spent in the cab of his truck, just him and miles of blacktop.

"So." His dad cleared his throat. "How long have the two of you been together?"

Jace nearly choked on his own tongue. Jerking up from his perch on the work bench, he forced words past a strangled wheeze. "What are you talking about?"

With his right hand, his dad scratched absently behind his left ear, effectively blocking his expression from Jace. "You and Quinn. How long have you two been seeing each other?"

His heart thumped erratically beneath his ribs. "We see each other about once a month." But his dad already knew that.

"That's not what I'm talkin' about and you know it."

Pushing off the car, his dad closed the distance between them. The man was tall, but still a couple of inches shorter than Jace. Although those inches didn't mean a damn thing when he set both hands on Jace's shoulders and stared straight into his soul.

"Your mother and I've both known for a while that you care about her, son. She's a good woman, the kind any man would be lucky to have in his life."

Jace just nodded. He couldn't do more with the heavy lump stuck in his throat.

"Whatever's going on between you, just know we want you both to be happy. And if that's together…" His voice trailed off before continuing. "Well, that would make your mama and I happy. Michael, too, if he were here."

The lump traveled, expanded.

"She doesn't have a daddy of her own, and for the last few years I've thought of her as my own. So don't take this the wrong way, son. But if you hurt her I'm going to have to hurt you. But don't worry. I have a feeling your mama's having pretty much the same conversation with her."

Jace groaned inside his own head. Great, Quinn was going to be even more wary now.

His dad slammed a heavy hand between Jace's shoulder blades and pulled him close.

Gruffly, he murmured, "I know you won't let anyone else hurt her, either."

DUE TO EVERYTHING that was happening, Daniel had told Quinn to take a few days off. The order had rubbed her the wrong way, but she realized he was probably right.

The last thing she wanted was to make trouble for the people who looked to them for help. Most of them were skittish enough to start with.

Jace seemed fairly certain Warren hadn't figured out who he was to Quinn—yet. The man had talked about her hiring a bodyguard. Which hopefully gave them a few days' breathing room until Warren put the pieces together.

Unfortunately, chances were he had eyes on the office and would pick up her trail as soon as she surfaced there. So for now she had to stay away.

So she'd postponed the cases that weren't critical and briefed other colleagues who would follow up on those that needed immediate attention. But there was one person she couldn't abandon—Caroline Warren.

When she'd placed her at the safe house, Quinn had promised Caroline she'd come back and see her. She wanted to give Caroline a steady and grounding presence. The two of them had bonded in the hours they'd spent together, and the last thing Caroline needed was Quinn abandoning her.

And, if Quinn were honest with herself, after everything that had happened in the past few days, she really needed to see the other woman. Not just to make sure Caroline was okay, but to remind herself why what she was doing was so important.

That the disruptions to her life were worth it.

Once again, she and Jace had argued about the idea. He thought it was a pointless risk. He didn't understand, and nothing she'd said to him could change his mind.

His priority was her safety, which Quinn understood and appreciated. But she refused to let Warren impact her life any more than he already had.

She couldn't put her life on hold indefinitely. There was no way to know when—or if—Warren would show up again. And eventually she'd have to return to normal, whether he made another move or not.

When Jace had realized she wasn't going to budge on this he'd reluctantly agreed with a few requirements of his own. One, they'd take a rental car so no one could trace them. She thought it was overkill, but whatever.

Two, they'd meet somewhere other than the safe house.

This made perfect sense to Quinn, since she wasn't just worried about keeping herself safe, but Caroline, as well.

So she was currently riding in a navy blue Nissan Maxima heading to a park on the outskirts of town. It was the middle of the day during the workweek. As they pulled into the small parking lot, Quinn took in the few people scattered around. Two mothers walked along the gravel path ringing the park, pushing strollers while they chatted. A handful of older kids were across the green space, playing a pick-up game of baseball.

In the center of everything sat a gazebo. It was a fairly large structure, made of light brown stone. Quinn knew that on summer weekends the town used the space to showcase local bands or put on craft fairs.

Today there were only two people sitting in the cool shadows beneath the structure.

Caroline Warren and Melanie, the woman who ran the safe house. Climbing up the steps, Quinn stopped long enough to give Melanie a hug. They'd known each other for years, and while they only seemed to see each other in the middle of some crisis, they'd formed a friendship. Even if it wasn't the kind that involved trips to the mall or late-night phone conversations.

"Sweetie." Melanie squeezed hard. "I hear you've bought yourself some trouble."

Quinn grimaced, but only allowed the reaction for the briefest moment. "Worth it."

Mel didn't have to voice her agreement, it was clear in the mixture of anger, resolve and understanding in her soft gray eyes.

Jace moved more slowly up the stairs, carefully studying their surroundings. Quinn had no idea what he was looking for, but decided to let him do whatever he needed to feel better about the situation. The gazebo was high and open on all sides, surrounded by a field. The closest person was at least thirty yards away, which meant they could speak without fear of being overheard.

It also meant no one could approach without being noticed.

Letting her go, Melanie crossed to Jace, offering her hand. "You must be Jace."

He took it, silently accepting the greeting, but not offering anything much in return.

Quinn sighed and fought the urge to roll her eyes. God, he could be a stubborn pain in the ass.

Leaving them, she crossed to the far side of the structure. Caroline, who'd been perched on the edge of one of the stone benches carved into the low wall, shot to her feet.

She started to reach for Quinn, but hesitated, her arms dropping back to her sides.

"I'm so sorry, Quinn," she whispered, the words coming out slightly broken.

Yeah, this wasn't going to do at all.

Closing the gap between them, Quinn wrapped the other woman in her arms. Caroline winced when Quinn accidentally hugged her bruised ribs too tightly, and Quinn tried not to let it fuel her fury again.

Pulling her back to the bench, Quinn sank to the hard, cool surface and urged her to do the same.

"You have nothing to apologize for. This isn't your fault, Caroline."

"Yes, but if I'd just stayed…" Her soft voice trailed off to nothing, her eyes going glassy with unshed tears.

"Oh, no you don't, lady. Leaving him was the right thing and everything he's done since then is more proof of that. Don't, for one second, entertain the thought that staying would have been a better option. Because that will seriously piss me off."

Caroline watched her for several seconds, her gaze scouring Quinn's, probably for some sign that she didn't mean what she'd just said. But she absolutely did. Every single word.

Getting Caroline away from that man was worth anything, including the disruption to Quinn's life.

No doubt Caroline had gotten pretty good at reading people, a result of the hypervigilance she'd developed in her abusive relationship. It was a valuable skill, especially when reading Warren well could spare her a beating.

Today, Quinn hoped Caroline could read her sincerity.

After several moments, a bright, beautiful smile stretched across Caroline's lips. It was such a transformation from the way Caroline had looked when Quinn had taken her to the safe house a handful of days ago that she couldn't help but respond with a smile of her own. It did her heart good to see Caroline doing so much better.

The heavy band that had been restricting her chest for days began to ease. This. This was why she did what she did. For these moments when it was obvious she'd helped someone who desperately needed it. When it was crystal clear that one person really could make a huge difference, even if only in one life.

Maybe *especially* when it was just one life.

Even Caroline's clothes had changed. Gone were the sophisticated designer dress, the expensive jewelry and the perfectly applied makeup she'd worn the last time Quinn had seen her. They'd been replaced with a loose-fitting pair of jeans and a pretty floral cotton shirt. Her hair was pulled back into an easy ponytail and she wore barely any cosmetics.

She looked younger. Definitely happier. Pretty.

"Freedom suits you."

Her words, meant as a compliment, had an unexpected effect. The light slowly drained from Caroline's green eyes and her skin went frighteningly pale.

"I'm worried about you, Quinn."

Quinn tried to brush the words away. "I've got good people looking out for me."

Caroline's gaze traveled across the space to where Jace stood at the entrance, facing away from them and staring off across the open field. "He's…big. And pretty. If a little intimidating."

"Pretty. That's not a word I'd use to describe Jace Hyland."

"Where'd you find him?"

"He's…" What was he? Not her almost brother-in-law, that was for sure. One night together did not make him her boyfriend. But she cared about him. And she knew he cared about her. Lover felt wrong, too dismissive of the history they shared.

"A friend," she finally said. "He's a good friend."

Caroline snorted, the sound startling Quinn. "I saw the way he watched you walk across the field. Dark. Intense."

"Annoyed?"

"Like if you weren't in a park surrounded by innocent children he'd have devoured you. Friend? Please, who are you trying to fool—me or yourself?"

Out of nowhere, heat suffused Quinn's skin. Damn freckles.

Caroline's eyes sharpened and a pleasant tinkle of laughter threaded between her lips. "I see," she said, dragging out the two words as if they held way more significance than normal.

Part of Quinn wanted to ask just what Caroline thought she'd seen. But Quinn managed to bite her tongue.

"We'll continue to communicate any necessary details through Melanie. Have you thought about what you want to do next? About pressing charges?"

Quinn hated to bring it up because she knew the reaction she'd get. But she wouldn't be doing her job—or doing Caroline any favors—if she didn't. Not to mention herself.

If Caroline pressed charges, Warren could go to jail and this entire fiasco would be over. Her life could return to normal.

Although, that thought didn't bring with it the kind of relief she'd expected.

If Warren wasn't a threat anymore there'd be no reason for Jace to stay with her. And then what?

All the laughter faded from Caroline's face leaving behind another glimpse of the broken woman she'd been a few days earlier.

"No, I haven't thought that far ahead. I know I can't go to my family, not if I want to keep them safe…or myself. That's the first place he'd look for me. California, maybe. Or Seattle. Far away."

"Far is good. Big cities are usually best—it's easier to blend in. There are channels that can help you start over, get you a new identity. Especially if you give the police the information you know about Warren's illegal activities."

Caroline nodded, looking down at the hands now clasped primly in her lap. Somewhere along the way, her posture had reverted from open and comfortable to jagged and perfect. Her ankles were crossed and tucked beneath the edge of the bench. Her head was bowed, her shoulders rounded and slumped.

Dammit.

"I don't think I can." Caroline looked up at her from beneath inky lashes, her eyes full of fear, pain and self-loathing. "I don't think I can be in the same room with him, Quinn, let alone look him in the eye while talking about what he did to me. And it isn't just him I'm worried about. The men he works for are powerful and dangerous. Maybe more dangerous than he is."

And they both knew that was saying a lot, considering the injuries Warren had given her.

Caroline's fingers slipped absentmindedly across the ragged scar that ran just above her wrist. Quinn hadn't asked, but she'd seen enough to be fairly certain it was from rope or leather or something else that had held Caroline captive at some point.

Her stomach churning, her lungs fighting for a full breath, Quinn covered Caroline's fingers and stilled them.

"There are people who can protect you, Caroline. You have to do what's best for you right now, but just promise me you'll think about it. If what you say is true, the authorities might offer you the most protection and the best chance at getting a new life. Better than if you run alone."

"I'm such a coward," Caroline whispered so softly that Quinn almost missed her words.

And she'd finally had enough. Slipping off the bench, Quinn knelt in front of her. She waited until Caroline met her gaze.

"You are not a coward. No one can fully understand what you've been through. There's no right or wrong answer here."

"But what if he hurts someone else because I couldn't make myself do it?"

Quinn wished there was something she could say to allay Caroline's fears. But there wasn't and she refused to lie to the woman.

"It's a possibility, but your first concern has to be for yourself. No one would blame you for that, not after what you've been through. Think about it, though."

Tears welled in Caroline's eyes, making them seem magnified. Several tears slid free, speeding down her cheeks one right after another.

She didn't sob or shake. She just let them silently roll. "Thank you, for everything you've done. You saved my life," Caroline said, her voice husky with emotion.

"You did that, Caroline, by having the strength to leave. I only helped a little. And I'd do it again in a heartbeat."

"No matter how much hell Everett puts you through?"

"A small price to pay for the smile you gifted me with a few minutes ago."

"I'll never be able to repay you."

"The best thank-you I could ever get is to know you're living a long and happy life."

The smile Caroline gave her this time was watery, but no less radiant.

"I think I can do that."

10

JACE HEARD QUINN'S heavy sigh. Out of the corner of his eye, he watched her sag against the beige leather seat. Exhaustion tightened the skin around her eyes and mouth, and not for the first time, he questioned whether the visit had been a smart idea.

Not because he thought it had put either Quinn or Caroline Warren in danger—because at the slightest indication of that he would have shut the whole thing down. But because it was obvious Quinn was internalizing this woman's pain and struggle, and had been doing it from the first moment.

He'd already known that—recognized the fierce protectiveness that sharpened her eyes when they'd fought over whether she needed protection in the first place. God, that felt as if it was weeks ago instead of days.

Quinn wasn't the only one exhausted.

The drive back to where he'd left his truck was a heck of a lot faster than their trip out to the park. On the way there he'd taken the time to back track and take false turns, although not once had he seen any indication that they'd been followed.

But he had the training so he'd taken the precaution.

Parking the rental car several rows away in the mall lot, Jace texted a buddy who was going to pick it up and deliver it back to the rental place in the morning. He could have taken it back himself, but the guy owed him and he wanted to get Quinn home where he felt she was safer.

Besides, taking it themselves would have meant separate vehicles. And there was something about the past few hours—maybe it was seeing the fear in Caroline Warren's eyes for himself… He needed to keep Quinn close.

With a hand to the small of her back, he guided Quinn across the lot. He scanned each line of cars as they went, searching for danger.

He tried not to be distracted by the way Quinn melted into his touch as if silently accepting the protective gesture. Welcoming it.

They were settled and pulling out of the lot when a shrill ringtone echoed through the cab. Quinn, who'd been staring sightlessly out the window, jumped. Without a word, she scrambled to pull out her cell phone.

A frown puckered the skin between her eyes. She flashed him a glimpse of the screen and the Unknown Number that scrolled across.

"Should I answer it?"

Jace hesitated. Something about it had the hairs on the back of his neck standing on edge, but it was probably better to know for sure than to wonder and worry.

Slowly, he nodded, pulling onto the shoulder of the road.

Taking a deep breath, Quinn accepted the call, placing it on speaker.

"Hello?" she asked, her voice quivering slightly although he was probably the only one who'd notice the miniscule sign.

"Ms. Keller."

What she couldn't hide was the soft gasp.

He couldn't help scanning the area around them again, though he knew they were alone. Warren had obviously gotten hold of Quinn's cell number, but that didn't necessarily mean he was lying in wait in the bushes along this random stretch of road.

A *tsking* sound whispered down the line. "You've been busy today. Did you tell my Caroline that I miss her? That I'm coming to take her home?"

Quinn's wide, panicked eyes flew to Jace. His hands gripped the steering wheel, knuckles white.

She was silently asking him what to do. The problem was he wasn't entirely certain himself.

His gut told him Warren was fishing. They'd taken enough precautions.

If the man truly knew where Caroline was, he wouldn't be wasting his time with this phone call. He'd already be at the safe house.

Jace gave a single, emphatic shake of his head. Quinn's eyebrows rose in silent question, but he didn't change his mind.

Quinn opened her mouth and carefully answered Warren's questions.

"I didn't see Caroline."

"Don't lie to me." Warren's harsh voice cracked across the cab of the truck. "You didn't go to work today. You haven't been home. But while you've been hiding, I've been doing my research, finding out everything I can about you. I'm so sorry for the loss of your parents. Such a difficult situation for one so young. Although your sister seemed to handle it well enough. You, on the other hand, struggled."

A strangled sound caught in the back of her throat. Jace looked over to find Quinn holding a hand to her mouth, trying to muffle her involuntary reaction from the monster trying to push all of her buttons.

If he hadn't already known just how strong Quinn was, that moment would have done it. Even without the story she'd shared with him last night, it was obvious how difficult this was. But she was doing whatever she had to in order to keep her cool and not let him get to her.

"You can't stay hidden forever, Ms. Keller. And neither can Caroline." Jace heard the barely leashed civility in his words. He was unraveling, the edge of insanity finally cutting through his facade. "Eventually you'll both have to reenter the world. And when you do I'll be there, waiting."

The line cut off, the silence of dead air almost worse than his taunting words.

With a shaking hand, Quinn reached for her phone and held the button down until the whole thing went dark, powered off.

Turning to him, she said, "Can I borrow your phone?" in a voice that was steadier than he'd expected.

Without hesitation, he handed it over. Her first call was to Melanie. They discussed the possibility of moving Caroline to another location, one with more security. The next call was to the lawyer handling Quinn's complaint and the last was to Daniel.

Jace listened, impressed with the calm, cool way she handled the situation. Not that he was really surprised.

He'd always known she had a backbone of steel and an IQ to back up that strength.

He also knew her well enough to realize that when everything was handled she was likely to give in to the temper building inside her. He could see evidence of it as her skin went from pale to bright pink. Her mouth thinned and the skin around her eyes tightened.

His hands contracted around the wheel as he stared out the windshield into the darkening night. Frustration and fear bubbled up inside him. They were impotent, and that only made the restless energy buzzing through him worse.

There was nothing for him to do.

He was used to tackling problems head-on. Drawing up tactical plans and executing. He was a man of action.

Tonight he felt useless, with Quinn's safety and Caroline's life hanging in the balance.

TENSION RADIATED OFF of him in waves. It made Quinn's own body tighten, as if her muscles were actually connected to his, affected by what he was feeling.

Quinn wanted to give him some relief, and she was desperate for a release to her own pressure, as well.

She was beyond pissed. An explosive mixture of emotions strung her body taut—frustration, anxiety, fury, impatience.

If something didn't give soon she was afraid she'd just start screaming and never be able to stop.

Jace ushered her up to his place, but just inside the door he said, "Stay here while I sweep the apartment."

She realized he was being smart and protective, but his harsh tone scraped across her already fraying nerves. Quinn watched him disappear, gun hanging loose and ready at his side.

How was she any safer next to the door than she would have been sitting on the sofa not ten feet away?

Shaking her head, Quinn dropped her arms, decided Jace was being overly dramatic, walked over and collapsed onto the soft cushions. The thing was massive, very masculine. She could easily tell where Jace preferred to sit because it dipped down into a comfortable impression.

Scooting over into that spot, she curled onto her side, pressing her cheek against the arm. For some reason it soothed her. As if Jace had his arms wrapped around her.

Quinn strained to hear any sign of him, but the apartment was silent. It shouldn't have surprised her, how light on his feet Jace was, but it did. Not even watching him bounce and shuffle in the ring had prepared her for the smooth, deadly way he could just…disappear.

"I thought I told you to stay by the door."

Quinn rolled her head back, letting her gaze move up his hips, fists planted firmly against them in irritation, over his chest, to his glaring eyes. At least he'd put the gun away.

It didn't bother her exactly, not when she realized its purpose was her protection. But the ease with which he handled the thing only emphasized to her the risks in his life. It was a reminder that he'd done and seen things she'd never understand.

She didn't like the reminder. Not even knowing he no longer spent his days knee-deep in danger could stop the sudden tightening in her chest whenever she thought of just how many times he'd brushed close to death.

Quinn had lost enough people in her life—to things most would call tragic and just plain bad luck—to realize terrible things happened all the time. She didn't hold a monopoly on pain and grief. In fact, she'd made a career out of helping others who were suffering, partly because it helped remind her that there were people out there dealing with much worse than she'd experienced.

But even the briefest thought that something could happen to Jace sent her heart thumping wildly and a sick wave of dread rolling through her stomach.

She tried to suppress the ill-timed reaction and her sudden need to touch him, hold him.

"I'm fine, Jace. And how is it safer for me over there than right here? It's been a long day and I just wanted to sit down."

His mouth thinned, but his eyes went soft. Closing the space between them, he dropped a hip to the edge of the couch beside her. Running the pad of his finger along her forehead, he smoothed several strands of hair off of her face.

"When I issue an order I need to know you're going to follow it."

"I'm not one of your soldiers, Jace. I don't have to blindly follow you."

His mouth quirked into a crooked smile that lacked an edge of humor. "You don't have to, but would it be too much to ask that you do it anyway?"

"Apparently," she said.

He sighed, his fingers dipping lower to trail beneath her jaw, tipping her face up so she was staring straight into his eyes. "What am I going to do with you?"

Heat rolled slowly through her body, replacing the sick sludge of emotions the day had left.

It wasn't the kind of wild spark she'd been struggling to control for the past two years. This was something more. Deeper. Easy and perfect.

Wetting her lips, she said, "I have a few ideas, but I'm open to suggestions."

An answering flare of need lit up his gaze. He shifted, his hip rubbing against her thigh. That one simple touch and she wanted to open for him, give him everything.

Stupid, stupid, stupid. But she couldn't seem to stop the compulsion.

His index finger slipped lower, down the slope of her throat and beneath the collar of her shirt. She'd never considered her collarbones an erogenous zone, but with him trailing tingles across her skin, it was hard to concentrate on anything else.

She wanted him to go lower. Her nipples tightened and ached. But he stayed right where he was and played. And she let him. It was too good not to.

Reaching out for him, she found the hard expanse of his thigh. God, the man was made entirely of rock-solid muscle. It shouldn't surprise her, the strength that lay hidden, but it did. It was easy to forget…until she touched him.

He watched her, those clear blue eyes going dark and just a little dangerous. Quinn squirmed beneath the sheer intensity of his scrutiny. The way he watched her made her feel like he could see straight through her. She was an open book—body, mind and soul. She couldn't keep any secrets, from him or herself, while he was watching her like that.

"God, I can't keep my hands off you, Quinn." The

sound of his low, gravelly voice was as much of a caress as his teasing fingers.

"Why do you have to?" she asked, so breathless she was afraid she'd start panting. She was a melting mass of need, a slave to her body and the response he was coaxing from her, while he was calm and controlled.

She wanted to affect him just as much.

"Because…my focus should be on protecting you."

She definitely didn't agree with him on that.

"That's bullshit and you know it. The only thing holding you back right now is the guilt, and I thought we'd laid that to rest yesterday."

He shook his head, staring mutely at her out of tortured eyes. She could see the fight, the pull against what his brain told him he should do and what his body was begging him to finish.

She knew which one she hoped won.

"What did your dad say to you?"

He blinked. "What?"

"Sam. What did he say to you when he dragged you out to the garage last night?"

She hadn't intended to bring up her conversation with Naomi. At the time she'd been embarrassed by it. Hadn't been ready to talk to Jace about it.

Now…maybe it was the one thing that could cut through the guilt.

And she wanted it gone.

"We weren't fooling them. Don't know about your dad, but Naomi saw right through us. The minute you guys left she started asking me questions."

He made a low warning sound that sent a surge of hope through her. Quinn quickly tamped it down. It meant nothing. Not really.

"I'm sorry, Quinn. We shouldn't have gone over there. Not yet."

"Don't you apologize to me. I knew what I was walking into. And I didn't mind. Do you know what she said to me, Jace? She said I would always be her daughter, no matter what happened between you and me. That she and your father loved me, Michael loved me and he'd be happy that I was finally happy."

The tears she'd fought at the time pricked the backs of her eyes again. She hadn't been ready to hear the words, but they were nice to have anyway.

She didn't know what this was or where they were going. But his mom was right—being with Jace made her happy. And for now, that was enough.

"Jace," she breathed out. "This feels right."

Sitting up, Quinn brought them face-to-face, inches apart. She could feel the humid warmth of his breath as it brushed across her cheek. Smell cinnamon and the barest hint of coffee. The heat of him overwhelmed her.

Slipping her hands beneath the hem of his tight black T-shirt, she ran her palms up and over his abs. She loved the way he responded to her touch, his muscles contracting in waves like ripples across water.

"It feels good, Quinn. There's a difference."

Suddenly, desire wasn't the only thing heating her blood; irritation burned with it. "Damn you, Jace. Is that what you think of me? That I'd chase physical pleasure and to hell with whatever destruction I left in my wake? Do you think I don't know how hard this is for you? That you're struggling with guilt over wanting me? That I haven't struggled with the same thing?"

His fingers gripped her shoulders, pulling her closer even as he tried to backtrack. "No, that's not what I meant. I know it's been a while for you, that's all. You're starting to move on and part of that is your body coming alive."

"There have been plenty of men over the last two years who would have been happy to accept an invitation to my bed. Men I was mildly attracted to. I could have had sex anytime I wanted, taking that physical comfort."

Quinn strained against his hold on her, not to get away but to push closer. His gaze bored into hers. She felt the impact of it straight down to her toes, but she wanted to make sure he heard her, saw the truth in what she was about to say.

"I've had love, Jace. I know there's more to sex than the physical. Do you think I'd settle for something cheap and fleeting after that? Do you think I'd cheapen what I had with him by accepting less?"

Jace drew in a sharp breath, but she didn't let his reaction slow her down.

"I'm not saying that's what we have. We do have more. I care about you and I always have. You're important to me, and not just because you were important to him. I see you. I want you. Not some random warm body in my bed. *You.*"

She watched him, waiting for some indication of his response. He simply stared at her, his eyes shuttered and unreadable.

And then he was surging against her, a low rumble rolling through his chest. Her back collided with the arm of the couch, arching her over and pushing her body high. He slid against her, chest to chest, hips to hips, until his mouth found hers and demanded she open and let him in.

As if she'd fight it. It's what she'd been fighting *for* the last ten minutes.

His fingers tangled in her hair, twisting and turning, moving her exactly where he wanted so he could taste and explore every corner of her mouth. All she could do was melt, take, accept and enjoy.

The man could kiss. Soft and slow, hard and sultry, he consumed her mouth in a way that made her feel as if kissing her was the only thing keeping him from breaking apart.

He poured every ounce of frustration, restless energy, fear and need into their joining. Quinn tasted it all, absorbing the firestorm and letting it twist through her own body.

She moaned, drawing in a desperate breath before diving under with him again. Her body writhed, wanting more. Could she burn up from just his mouth?

With Jace anything was possible.

His hands ran beneath the hem of her shirt, dragging it up her body. One hand spread across her back, his fingers so wide they practically spanned her shoulder blades. Biceps bulging, he held her up so he could toss her shirt away. In the back of her head, she heard it hit something with a soft swish.

An arm wrapped tight around her ribs, Jace shifted them. One moment she was on her back, the next she was upright and straddling his lap.

His hold on her didn't loosen as he pressed her fully against him. Needing skin on skin, Quinn quickly pulled his shirt off. She was afraid they were both going to be consumed by the heat burning between them.

But what a way to go.

His mouth trailed down her neck and across the collarbones he'd been so taken with earlier. Shivers followed in his wake.

Quinn's fingers tightened in the hair at the back of his neck, holding them both in place. The questing tip of his tongue dipped beneath the edge of her bra, drawing a surprised gasp.

She reached behind her, fumbling for the clasp that would free her for more, but a single hand grasped her wrists and closed around them tight. Behind her back, his hold arched her body, driving her breasts higher.

It didn't hurt, but put her already tumbling world more off kilter. Being unable to use her hands only made her want to touch him more.

Then his mouth settled across her aching nipple. He sucked, hard, drawing her deep into his mouth. Even through the barrier of satin, it was almost too much. He licked and sucked, teeth scraping against her puckered flesh, drawing a gasp from her as deep inside her core pulsed with growing need.

He paid the same attention to the other side, leaving her panting and squirming. She writhed, grinding their hips together in an effort to find some relief for the building ache. But it wasn't enough.

Not when they were both still wearing way too many clothes.

"Jace. Please. Take them off."

She could feel his lips curve against her skin. "Take what off?"

"All of it. Now." From her vantage point, a little above him, she stared down, compelling him to give her what she wanted.

His gaze sharpened, going dark and predatory. His hips shifted up, even as his heavy hands held her in place, grinding against her and giving her what she needed—almost but not quite.

Releasing his hold on her wrists, he snapped the clasp of her bra and swept it off her shoulders. It fell to the cushions beside them, completely forgotten. Hands cupping her hips, he set her back onto her feet.

Quinn swayed, her head swimming. He kept hold of her, using one hand to keep her upright while the other worked her zipper. She might have been a little fuzzy, but there were two things standing between her and bliss—her pants and Jace's jeans. And she wanted both gone. Quickly.

Hooking her thumbs into the waistbands of her jeans and panties, Quinn shoved. With a flick of each ankle, she sent her flats skittering across the floor. Her jeans were barely an abandoned pile at her feet before she was leaning over and tugging at the buttons on his fly.

He hissed when her fingers scraped down the long ridge of his erection, but he didn't stop her. His own hands fell to the couch, gripping the cushions like an anchor locking him in place. His hips rose before she'd popped the last metal disc free. It was all the invitation she needed, tugging at the tight denim until it slithered down his thighs to pool at his feet.

Kneeling, she yanked at the heavy boots he preferred. Dangerous men and their footwear. Shaking her head, Quinn tossed one over her shoulder and then the other, not caring if the steel-reinforced boots broke anything on their way down.

She'd barely gotten him free before his hands were spanning her waist again, pulling her back onto his lap.

This time, she was the one hissing when the blazing heat of him touched her clammy, needy skin.

Her thighs bracketed his. Her sex slid against him, searching for that perfect angle that would finally bring them together. But Jace held her away, keeping her from sinking onto him.

He used their friction against her, dragging her body across him, even as his thighs widened and urged her open more.

His thumb slipped between the lips of her sex, playing and teasing. God, she didn't think she could take much more. Not tonight.

He rubbed her clit, bringing her close before backing off. Her hips thrust against him, searching, hoping, begging for more.

And then he was spreading her open, the heavy head of his sex probing at her entrance. Her body clenched tight, wanting, needing him to fill her.

He tried to give it to her slowly, torturing them both inch by inch, but Quinn wasn't in the mood to wait.

Rolling her hips, she dropped down, taking him all in one smooth, deep stroke. His hand, caught between them, ground against her clit and nearly sent her straight into orbit. But she wasn't ready to let go, not yet.

Quinn went still, relishing the way they fit together. Her body pulsed around him, fluttering with the orgasm she was forcibly holding back. Her eyes closed for a moment as she savored the sensation of him filling her.

At her hips, his fingers tightened, digging in and holding her hard. His head dropped against the back of the couch, his eyes glassy with pleasure. Pleasure she'd given him. Power and satisfaction rolled through her.

Deliberately, she tightened her internal muscles, eliciting a groan that rocketed straight through her. "Are you trying to kill me?" he asked, his words fractured and desperate.

"Not until I'm done with you," she promised. "God, you feel so good."

"Babe, you gotta move." He backed up the words with his big hands, trying to force her hips to rock against him.

She thought about keeping herself rigid, not giving him what he wanted. But that would torture her as much as him, and she didn't have that kind of control. Not right now.

Giving in, Quinn rocked up onto her knees, letting him slowly slide free of her body.

A moan dragged up from the depths of her lungs as she sank down, once again taking him in all the way. Back and forth. Up and down. She rode him, each successive retreat and plunge going deeper, harder. His hips surged against her, meeting her thrust for thrust.

The couch creaked. The squeal of the legs against wood told her they were so frenzied the furniture was moving. She didn't give a damn. And apparently neither did he.

Her hands gripped the back of the sofa, trying to find that last little bit of leverage that would vault her into oblivion. Her body was strung so tight, she was afraid if she didn't get relief the only alternative was to break into a million pieces.

And then it was there, rushing at her, exploding out from the bottom of her spine to curl her toes and pull a cry straight from her soul.

Jace was right there with her, arms wrapped around her, holding her tight as his hips surged those last few times. She could feel the kick of him deep inside, the swell of his release only prolonging hers.

When reality finally returned, it was a bit of a shock.

Quinn glanced around them and realized they'd moved the couch several feet.

They were sweaty, their skin clinging together and reluctant to let go. Jace held her tight, his face buried deep in the crook of her neck. His breath, still strained, puffed in ragged draws against her cooling skin. The sensation over her still-sensitive nerve endings had delicious prickles spreading across her shoulders and arms.

Her gaze landed on a pair of buggy eyes staring at her out of a squished little face. Bacon's fluffy tail swished lazily back and forth across the end table she was perched on several feet away.

Quinn's body jolted. Jace tightened his hold on her.

"What's wrong?" he asked, his voice still gruff with the aftermath of exertion.

Quinn just shook her head. "Your cat is creepy."

They both turned to watch as Bacon daintily picked her way across the furniture over to them and curled her body into a ball on the back of the sofa, right next to Jace's head.

"She isn't my cat."

Quinn smothered a laugh. "I don't think anyone's explained that to her."

"Trust me," he grumbled, "I've tried."

Bacon reached out a paw and began to lick it, completely ignoring them. It was almost like she'd been politely waiting for them to finish so she could move in.

The way Quinn figured it, she had two choices: let a tiny cat chase her away, or ignore her.

Considering she didn't really want to move—ever—she went with option two.

There was a quiet in the aftermath. A peace.

They weren't fighting against themselves or each

other. In that moment nothing else mattered. Not what was happening outside or down the street or on the other side of the world.

It was the two of them, together.

Or it should have been.

11

PICKING HER UP, Jace carried her down the hall to his bed. They'd shared it last night, but this was different. There was still a part of him that felt like he was...taking something that wasn't his.

It didn't feel wrong, but it didn't quite feel right, either.

Although, when he was touching her it was hard to think about anything else. And Quinn didn't let him put much space between them. When he tried to pull back and recover some distance, she simply grabbed him and rolled, pillowing her head on his chest and tangling their limbs together.

What was he supposed to do?

His hands settled into the curve of her waist and the swell of her hip.

She let out a small, contented sigh that somehow both soothed him and ratcheted his tension higher. Within a few minutes the even drag of her breath told him she was asleep. Which was good. She'd had a rough couple of days.

He wasn't so lucky.

His muscles tightened, slowly winding beneath the pressure of the tension trying to claim him. It could have been minutes or hours, he wasn't certain.

When her phone rang, he was so taut he nearly vaulted off the bed.

Quinn made a confused, mewling sound, her lashes fluttering before finally opening to reveal dazed eyes.

"What?" she asked, her voice sleepy.

Going up on an elbow, Jace reached over her to the bedside table. "It's your cell."

He'd plugged it in to charge and turned it back on for her while she was washing her face and getting ready for bed. "Huh?" she asked, even as he shoved the thing into her hands. She hit the green button, probably more out of habit than true intent.

Jace could tell the moment her brain kicked in, clearing out the last cobwebs of sleep. She bolted straight up in bed. His sheets slithered down her body to pool at her waist. Soft moonlight slid across her pale, freckled skin. Jace wanted to lean forward and press his mouth to the tiny spots.

But the expression on her face stopped him.

Shock. Loss. Followed quickly by crystal-clear anger.

Her voice was smooth as steel and just as hard when she said, "Give me ten or fifteen minutes and we'll be there. Thank you."

She ended the call, but stared at the phone for several moments, stunned by whatever news it had delivered. Jace half expected the thing to just melt into a useless lump of plastic beneath the fire of her glare.

He reached for her, running his hands softly across her shoulders and down her back. "What's wrong?"

She turned her head and Jace's hands stilled. His

shoulders bunched and within seconds he was bounding off the bed, ready to kill whoever had put that expression on her face. All he needed was for her to point him in the right direction.

"That was the police. Someone broke into my house. Trashed it."

"Trashed it?"

She nodded. "They didn't give me details but…I've heard enough cops deliver bad news. Thank God, no one's dead, but he said it in that same tone of voice. It isn't good."

Reaching into a drawer, Jace jerked out a pair of jeans and a T, and was dressed in record time. Quinn was ready right beside him, her mouth a tight, unhappy line.

They reached the bedroom door together, but before she could go through, he snagged her arm and cradled her to him.

Gently, his mouth found hers. The move was pure instinct, the need to soothe her. At first she was stiff, maybe surprised, but within a couple of beats she was melting against him.

Jace felt the swarm of emotion she'd been fighting unfurl through her muscles. Her arms wrapped around him as she pressed soft curves into his hard body. She let the heat and comfort he was offering sink in deep, accepting what he was trying to give her—something good to think about instead of what they were headed toward.

After several minutes he slowly pulled away. She blinked up at him, the anger and irritation replaced by a dreamy haze. Unfortunately, it didn't last long and he had to watch it melt away again.

"Dammit," she finally whispered, burying her head in his chest.

"You're fine. We'll get him."

A harsh sound scraped through her throat. "At the moment, everyone better hope the cops get to him before I do."

Jace bit back a scoffing sound of his own. Like he'd let Warren close enough for her to do anything to the man. Because if she was close enough to hurt him, Warren was close enough to hurt her.

GOD, HER PLACE was a wreck. More than a wreck. Every piece of glass had been smashed—windows, mirrors, glasses, picture frames. Even the tiny crystal Eiffel Tower Michael had brought her back a trip to Europe when they'd first started dating.

Her clothes had been thrown out of the closet and dresser. But that hadn't been enough. The bastard had taken a pair of scissors and ripped into every single piece she owned.

Someone had slashed straight through her mattress. Sharp pieces of coiled metal stuck up where her body should have been. The thought sent a shiver down her spine.

Every piece of furniture she owned was either smashed or broken. A few of the more solid pieces looked as if they'd been chopped up with an ax, angry slashes of scarred wood shining through the veneer of polish and stain.

When the call had come in she'd only been pissed. There hadn't been room for much more. But it had only taken her a few minutes of shuffling through the debris of her life for that to be overshadowed by fear.

Which only pissed her off more.

How had she become a hostage in her own life?

"Where the hell is he?" Jace's voice rose from where he stood with one of the cops in the corner of her living room.

A handful of other officers milled around. Their movements looked random, although Quinn was certain they had a purpose. They wouldn't wander aimlessly through her broken house in the middle of the night for shits and giggles.

Jace's face was thunderous as he looked around, cataloguing the destruction of her home. Fists rolled into tight balls at his sides, he stared at the officer in front of him.

Quinn had been on the receiving end of that intense gaze on more than one occasion. It had been intimidating enough then. But now that it was full of impotent rage, she felt sorry for both men.

Thinking to defuse the situation, she moved in their direction.

His voice was hard, a low, dangerous rumble. "This is the third time this man has threatened her. What does he have to do before someone arrests him?"

Another officer strolled purposely toward them. Good, more reinforcements. "Trust me, we'd like nothing better. Given Ms. Keller's previous complaint, Mr. Warren has already received a visit from us."

"Fabulous," Jace ground out between his teeth.

Reaching the little group, Quinn placed a hand on Jace's arm. He dropped her a quick glance and then jerked his attention back to the two men in front of him. But his other hand settled over hers and squeezed.

He was upset, but not on the edge. She'd experienced

that moment enough herself to recognize the signs and he wasn't there.

Actually, looking around at the mess once more, she was surprised she wasn't close to losing her temper. A few days ago she definitely would have been. Worrying about keeping Jace calm had given her something to focus her attention.

"Mr. Warren has an alibi. There's no way he's responsible for the break-in."

"Having an alibi doesn't equal not responsible. Especially with his money and connections."

One of the officers frowned, deep grooves bracketing his mouth. Reaching up, he rubbed a heavy hand across his neck, bending beneath the weight.

"We realize that. But it'll take time for us to prove that and connect the dots."

"She could be dead by then," Jace growled. "Do you know what his next move might be?" He didn't wait for a response. "No, neither do I, but I know I don't really want to find out. He's getting more aggressive. This was a message, destroying the things she cares about and demonstrating he can get to her anytime he wants."

Both men shifted uncomfortably. Jace wasn't saying anything they hadn't already realized, but they didn't particularly like that *he* knew it.

"We're doing the best we can, Mr. Hyland."

"That's not enough. What's it going to take? Her ending up bloody and bruised like his poor wife?"

"No." The single word was emphatic. "She's already got 24/7 protection from you. We can place a unit outside your place as backup."

For the first time, Quinn broke into the conversation. "For how long? I've already put my life on hold.

I have a job. People depending on me. I can't hole up indefinitely."

"No, ma'am. But at least for a few days. We can re-evaluate then, see if the threat has changed."

Quinn cursed under her breath. She couldn't help but feel that hiding was the equivalent of letting him win.

The radio on one officer's shoulder squawked. He pushed a button and spoke, walking several feet away. The other officer went back to whatever he'd been doing.

They went about their jobs, but she could tell Jace was still struggling to contain the fury rolling through him.

It was hard not to appreciate his reaction, the protective streak that had him wanting to take care of her and the entire situation.

Sighing, she shuffled through the wreckage to the center of her den.

Staring at the window frame and the plywood Jace had nailed up to cover the opening left by the baseball, Quinn said, "Guess I need to call the window guy and tell him I need more than one repaired now."

She could feel Jace, the radiating heat and sheer physical presence of him, when he stepped up beside her.

"I'm so sorry, Quinn."

She shrugged. "Not your fault." What else was there to say?

"No, but I hate seeing your home this way. It must hurt."

She swiveled her head, taking in the destruction. She'd expected it to hurt. And, yes, there were things she was disappointed to lose, but they were things.

She'd learned a long time ago, things weren't as important as the people you shared them with.

Shrugging again, she answered, "Not really."

He pivoted, glass crunching and grinding beneath his feet.

"What do you mean?" he asked. He stared at her as if she'd gone mad. Or maybe as if she *could* go mad at any moment, finally cracking beneath the pressure.

Funny, she didn't feel under pressure.

"Yes, it's going to be a pain in the rear to get everything replaced, but…they're just things."

"Things you and Michael shared. This was your home together."

Quinn looked his way, although her body remained pointing away from him.

She took him in, all barely leashed power and vitality. He was brimming with energy and the need to do something. To fix and protect.

Apparently he still hadn't learned you couldn't save everyone. Or everything.

It was a realization she'd come to long ago.

"Michael hasn't been here in a very long time, Jace."

Her words were soft, although she knew that wouldn't make them hurt less.

"How can you be so calm?" His voice rose, drawing stares again. Leaning down, he picked up a piece of something she couldn't identify and dropped it back down again. It broke into a few more pieces, but Quinn didn't care.

It didn't matter. Broken was broken—two, five or twenty thousand pieces didn't make a difference.

"How can you be so upset? These aren't even your things."

"That asshole paid someone to break in here and destroy your home, your sanctuary. The place you shared with Michael."

"No. He paid someone to break in and rip apart a few inanimate objects. It's my choice whether or not I let him steal something more. And I refuse to give him that power."

Jace stared at her, eyes wide with confusion. "I don't understand you," he ground out.

I know, she thought, but didn't say it. Instead, Quinn walked away. She couldn't force him to see it from her perspective.

"If you'd been here. You could have been hurt. Seriously hurt."

And suddenly, she understood. Anxiety and fear. She'd struggled with that debilitating concoction herself after her parents died, constantly worried about who else could be stolen from her life.

Eventually, she'd realized that the worry was wasted energy. She couldn't stop it, if it was going to happen. She hadn't been able to save Michael or prevent her grandmother from having a heart attack. It was out of her control.

The only thing she could do was be grateful for each day she had with the people that mattered.

Closing the space between them, Quinn rose up on her toes. Hands bracketing his face, she found his mouth and placed a soft, soothing kiss there. "But I wasn't," she whispered. "You were protecting me, Jace."

THE DRIVE BACK to Jace's place was heavy with unspoken words. The weight of his silence pressed across her chest. They were both lost deep inside their own heads. Part of her really wanted to know what he was thinking.

The rest of her feared it would just make a difficult night even more untenable.

Opening her car door, Jace silently waited for her to get out. His tall, strong body towered above her. The heat of him radiated up and down her spine, a delicious sensation that had her melting before he'd even touched her.

She didn't have to watch him to know his gaze was darting around the dark parking lot, searching for any sign of a threat. The black metal of his gun was nestled in his palm, ready and waiting.

Quinn sighed, suddenly exhausted by everything that had been happening for the past few days. It was late. Or early. Closer to dawn than midnight, for sure. She'd just lost all of her possessions and it would probably be weeks before her home was habitable again.

Slumping against the wall right inside the door, she let Jace do his hunt and destroy mission through the apartment. Letting her head fall back, she closed her eyes and just listened.

A few days ago she couldn't pick out a single sound as Jace moved through the place. Tonight she was hyperaware of him. The barely audible swish of his shoes against carpet. The squeak of a floorboard under his weight. His fingers pushing open a door.

Behind closed eyelids, she could see the way his body moved, the give and take of muscles as they rippled. His strength and focus. The intensity burning deep inside his blue eyes.

She was so afraid that one day the intensity was going to burn her up. Or burn out. It was the situation.

Sure, Jace had said he'd wanted her for a long time, but he'd been able to deny himself. Until now. Protecting her had pushed some buttons deep inside.

But it couldn't last. This wouldn't last.

Eventually she'd lose. Again. How often was she destined to end up alone?

Unbidden, tears stung her eyes. Clamping her jaw shut, she forced them back. Not now. Not tonight. God, she'd held it together at the house. She didn't want to lose it now.

She had to be strong. She always had to be strong.

But apparently tonight she just didn't have any more to give.

Quinn didn't realize she was actually crying until something soft brushed against her cheek. Her eyes popped open and she found Jace standing in front of her, staring at her bleakly.

She felt the same hollowness inside. But tonight she knew they could fill the empty spaces for each other.

Leaning forward, Jace pressed his warm lips just beneath her eye. Her lids fluttered but didn't close. He kissed away her tears one by one. The gesture left her with the sweetest ache.

"I'm sorry," he whispered against her skin, pressing his lips against her jaw, forehead, nose and chin.

"For what?"

"Everything. That he's hurting you."

How could she tell him Warren had nothing to do with the tears she was shedding? Quinn just shook her head, unable to form the right words to explain.

"That I hurt you."

Maybe she didn't need words after all.

He tried to say more, but Quinn placed a finger

against his mouth, silencing him. "Shh." Pushing up on tiptoes, she fused her lips with his.

What he'd given her was sweet and delicate. What she gave to him was fluid energy. The very beginnings of passion. That edge right before the crackle erupted beneath her skin and restless anticipation took over.

Jace groaned, his hands cradling the back of her head and pulling her closer. His fingers tangled in her hair, tightening. He moved into her, pressing her back against the wall. She loved the way he surrounded her, all hard muscle. The reminder that even beneath this honeyed moment he was barely leashed strength and delicious excitement.

But tonight, that wasn't enough. She wanted more from him. Slipping out from beneath his body, she grasped his hand and led him down the hallway to his bedroom.

Stopping in the center of the room, Quinn turned to face him. He didn't say anything, but he didn't have to. There was a bright light in the back of his eyes, a fire that she could feel racing across her own skin.

She trembled, her entire body quivering beneath the weight of his need for her. It was heady and scary. But Quinn had never been the kind of person to back down out of fear.

He made a move to close the space between them, but with a quick shake of her head Quinn stopped him.

His gaze sharpened, turning predatory, but he stayed right where he was. His fists clenched at his sides, proof of just what it was costing him to give her this.

That tight control only made her want him more. Made her want to see just what it would take to break the hold he had on his actions and emotions.

Crossing to him, she grasped the hem of his shirt and in one fluid motion pulled it off. His head bent so that he could watch her, but he stayed still. The only thing that touched her was his fiery gaze.

A shiver rocked through her body.

Her palms played across his skin, a tingle shooting up from her fingertips. He was hot to the touch, smooth and silky.

She wanted more.

Letting her hands trail down, she relished the hitch in his breath as her fingers slipped beneath the waistband of his jeans. He hadn't bothered with boxers when they'd both scrambled to find clothes and race out the door earlier, and now she was grateful.

Especially when the swollen head of his penis brushed against the backs of her fingers. A groan rumbled up through him. Quinn thought about pressing her mouth to his chest so she could feel his pleasure reverberate through her own body.

But uncovering him was more tempting.

Tugging at his button and zipper, she slowly peeled away the denim separating them. God, he really was beautiful. Hard and heavy with his need for her.

Her own body reacted immediately, a liquid fire burning and aching at the center of her sex. She wanted him there, filling her, moving slowly and driving away absolutely every thought but how amazing he could make her feel.

Dropping to the floor in front of him, she unlaced his boots and made quick work of tossing them behind her. Even before the second one had hit the dresser with a thud, he was kicking his jeans off.

And Quinn couldn't tear her gaze from him.

She wanted to touch and taste, pull him deep into her mouth.

Her tongue darted out, wetting her lips in unconscious reaction to the thoughts rampaging through her brain. Jace groaned, his hands weaving through her hair again.

Quinn leaned back, letting her gaze travel up him. From her vantage point, she had the perfect view of his well muscled body. Yes, he was gorgeous, but that wasn't what had her so turned on she could barely catch a full breath—not that she didn't appreciate the package.

It was the way he watched her. Cradled her head in his powerful hands as if she was the most precious thing he'd ever touched, and didn't demand a single thing from her. Which only made her want to give him everything.

But she wasn't done torturing him.

Pushing up from the floor, she took several steps away. He reached out, trying to keep her close, but she evaded him.

Tugging her own T-shirt over her head, Quinn let her hair rain down around her shoulders. She reached behind her, flicking open her bra clasp. The straps slid down her arms, the sensation of satin against her tingling skin almost more than she could bear. Jace's hungry gaze latched onto one bra strap, following the torturously slow descent, stoking her need higher.

His ribs expanded and contracted beneath the smooth expanse of his tanned skin.

The scrap of satin and lace she'd been holding hit the floor. Jace swallowed, his throat convulsing.

There was something so…powerful about the moment. A gift they were sharing. And he hadn't even touched her yet. But she felt the pressure of it, an ever-strengthening band twining tighter between them, drawing them closer.

Quinn tugged at the button of her fly and then her zipper. The rasp of metal teeth was loud in her ears. Digging her thumbs into the loosened waistband, she dragged her shorts and panties down in one swift motion. They pooled at her feet, instantly forgotten.

Quinn stood in front of him fully naked, enjoying the tortured groan Jace couldn't quite hold back.

It was heady, knowing she could make him want her so badly.

Taking a single step, Quinn closed the space between them. Jace's hands settled on the curve of her waist, digging in and pulling her closer.

His face buried in the crook of her shoulder. She expected him to kiss her there. Instead, he simply inhaled.

"God, you always smell so good."

Her skin pebbled at the sound and feel of his words.

She wasn't just standing before him physically naked. She was baring much more than her body. Without realizing it, she'd started revealing her soul. And maybe taking a piece of his in return.

Quinn worshipped him with hands, lips and tongue. She wanted to touch every part of him. To feel and measure, cherish and discover.

This wasn't the broken dam of physical need their first joining had been. Or the carnal frenzy of earlier. It was more. Profound in a way that had a lump of tears gathering again at the back of Quinn's throat.

The way he looked at her…it sent shivers through her body. As if she was the only thing preventing him from drowning. As if there wasn't a single thing about her he didn't want and need.

As if he was finally free and she was the one who'd given him the key.

When he scooped her up in his arms, a muffled squeal of shock fell from her lips. Kneeling on the bed, he set her gently onto the soft gray sheets before stretching out beside her.

He propped himself on one elbow, letting his fingers play up and down her body. She was spinning, her world tilting off its axis.

She tried to roll into him, to bring them together, but a heavy hand spread in the center of her stomach held her in place. He teased and tortured, brushing calloused fingertips over her body.

His talented fingers plucked at her aching nipples, rolling and soothing before bringing them back to a sharp point of need. He pressed his mouth to her shoulder, kissing and biting his way up to her throat.

His tongue rimmed her ear as he blew a soft breath against her dampened skin. The base of her spine tightened with a restless ball of energy that just kept growing and growing.

She had no idea how long he teased her with caresses that were never enough. But by the time his hands and mouth moved lower she was already writhing, her body silently begging.

She was a mass of raw nerves and need searching for the relief only he could give her.

Flattening her palm against his chest, she could feel the racing beat of his heart thumping furiously against her palm. The heat rolling off of him seared her skin. Her hand traveled down, over the swell of his pecs to his abs and ribs. She brushed against the black ink curling across his stomach and the raised ridges of tissue hidden beneath. For the first time the reminder didn't make her inwardly cringe. It only made her need worse.

God, this man was perfect in so many ways—inside and out.

The heavy weight of his hand settled over hers. Staring straight into her eyes, he directed her hand lower. Quinn sucked in a harsh breath, unable to look away from him, not even to watch what they were doing.

As she wrapped her fingers tight around the jutting hardness of his erection, he sandwiched her hand between his velvety smooth shaft and his firm palm. Jace's eyes slipped closed and his head tipped back as a deep groan dragged past his parted lips.

Quinn began to stroke him. Up and down, slow and hard. Her hips pumped in time to their rhythm, unconsciously seeking more for herself even as she was completely absorbed with the thrill of watching him come undone.

Out of nowhere warm fingers skated up the inside of her thigh. She jumped, startled at the unexpected contact, but quickly sank into the sensation. He easily found the throbbing, aching heart of her. And, God, his touch felt so damn good.

As her thighs dropped open, Quinn's hips arched upward, silently asking for more. She wanted. *Needed.*

Jace traced fingers around her opening, teasing her sensitive flesh. He found her clit and rubbed, driving her straight to the brink.

She ached. Throbbed. Whimpered, the needy sound clawing at the back of her throat.

And then he was plunging two fingers deep inside,

stretching and rubbing and making her pant in desperation.

Matching the stroke of his fingers to the slide of their joined hands around his sex, all Quinn could think about was how it would feel if he was deep inside her.

Her body craved the images her mind conjured up.

"Please," she groaned, unable to keep her hips from pumping hard against his hand. Her mind wanted him, but her body was greedy enough to take relief in any form.

"What, beautiful? Tell me what you want."

"You!" she cried. She was so close, forcibly holding off her release. But she couldn't do it for long.

Jace reared away from her. Quinn nearly sobbed out her frustration when everything stopped. Until he shifted, pressing her deep into the bed. She could feel him, nudging at her entrance, and she just wanted him there already.

Digging her fingers into his rear, Quinn rocked up at the same time she drove him down. They slipped together like a key into a lock. Relief and peace stole through her.

How could anything that felt this right be wrong? It couldn't. She and Jace were perfect together.

He groaned, his mouth finding her ear. "I'll always give you what you need, Quinn. Always."

And then he was moving. They were both past the point of slow and easy. Pleasure spiked through her over and over again. She wrapped her legs high around his waist and used the leverage to meet him thrust for desperate thrust.

Together, they strained for that one, pure, perfect

moment they could share. She knew it was there, shimmering just out of reach.

His hips pistoned against hers. Sweat and need mixed on his skin. The mingled tastes burst across her tongue when she latched onto the base of his throat and sucked. A low, tortured sound rumbled up through his chest.

Quinn closed her eyes, her vision going black with starbursts of bright color. And then everything was on fire—her body, the world around them. It rampaged through her, stealing her breath, forcing out a strangled cry of relief.

Somewhere in the back of her brain Quinn realized she'd lost control of her body. She was shaken by the force of her release. The only thing that kept her grounded were Jace's arms tight around her.

And then he was yelling her name. She could feel his release. Loved knowing he was buried deep, losing himself in her.

Wrapping her arms tight around him, Quinn cradled him with her body. His shoulders shook, arms trembling from the strain of keeping the full weight of his body off her.

But she wanted it. Wanted all of him. Tugging, she relished the way he gave and collapsed onto her.

His labored breaths sounded in her ear. His racing heart beat right beside her own less-than-steady pulse. Their fevered bodies slid together, settled.

It could have been three minutes or thirty, Quinn had no idea. But soon her sweat-slicked skin got chilled. Still, she didn't want to move. Not when Jace was tracing mindless patterns along her shoulder and arm.

She was happy. Content. If someone had offered her

the chance to freeze the moment and live inside it forever, Quinn would have taken it.

And then Jace had to go and ruin it.

"We lost him today, two years ago."

12

THE DATE WAS permanently etched into Jace's psyche…
right along with the ink covering the scars below his
ribs.

It was the day he'd lost a piece of himself. No, given
it freely, only to have a bigger piece of his life torn
away instead.

A tight band tried to cut off his supply of oxygen.
No, wait, that was the weight of Quinn's hand heavy
against his chest.

"Don't," she whispered.

They were still joined. Out of nowhere, guilt and
grief tried to choke him. What was he doing?

His fingers clamped around her hips, ready to lift her
away. But she wouldn't let him put space between them.

Instead, her legs and arms wrapped around him,
holding tight. "Don't," she whispered. "Do not use his
memory like this, Jace."

He just shook his head. "I don't know what you're
talking about."

"Bullshit," she spit out, her gorgeous brown eyes
flashing fire.

He watched her, unable to look away. Or fight her hold on him. A single question plagued him. God, he didn't really want the answer, but couldn't stop himself from asking, "Do you still miss him?"

She didn't hesitate. "Absolutely."

Her answer cut into him with sharp precision. It was exactly what he deserved. He'd been playing with fire for days and this was the price.

The thing was, even knowing he should, he wouldn't have done a single thing differently. Having her here with him was worth any amount of pain that would come afterward.

"But a little less every day," she continued.

Turning her gaze upward, she stared at the ceiling. Or maybe she was looking a little higher.

"I miss the way his eyes would crinkle at the edges when he laughed. Or the exasperation that crept into his voice whenever I'd do something stupid like load the dishwasher and forget to turn it on. Or his will to fight until the very end."

Jace felt a hitch in the center of his chest. A heavy breath that sliced him open instead of setting him free.

He missed all of those things. And so many more. The way Michael had whined when he was eight or nine and Jace had picked on him. Or that mischievous sparkle, and the way he'd tilt his head to the side when he was trying to get away with a lie.

He needed space. Air. Something.

No, he needed his little brother back, but that wasn't going to happen.

His grip on Quinn's hips tightened. He wasn't sure if it was to push her away or pull her closer. Not anymore. His brain didn't even know what the right thing was.

He'd lost that certainty, drowning in her scent and taste and just the comforting, igniting feel of her so close.

He'd been floating. For two years his feet had been firmly planted on the ground and still he'd been floating. And he hadn't even realized it until she'd pulled him back and grounded him. Given him something more than the unimportant things he'd forced himself to get up for every day.

He couldn't let her go. Not now. Not ever.

God, if he lost her…

Irrational fear stampeded through his body, leaving him breathless and feeling as though a few vital organs had been crushed along the way. His grip tightened further, turning her flesh angry pink beneath his hold. His eyes registered it. Knew he should ease up.

But he couldn't do it.

As if sensing just how close he was to losing it, Quinn shifted. She folded her body, although somehow managing to keep them joined together.

"It's a day, Jace. No more important than yesterday or tomorrow. An opportunity to remember how he touched our lives, but Michael wouldn't want you using it to dwell and mourn. Or push me away."

They were connected in the deepest way two people possibly could be—not just physically, but emotionally.

She saw too much, understood him better than probably anyone else ever had. Expect maybe his little brother.

Without meaning to, he'd ripped himself wide open for her, spilling out all the darkness he tried to keep hidden right along with the light.

Quinn was staring at him, luminous and brilliant,

looking as if she could cherish what he'd given instead of running screaming.

Restless energy buzzed through him. It wasn't arousal. Or not just arousal. It was gratitude and appreciation. Awe and humility. Devotion and the knowledge that she was going to challenge and push every single one of his buttons. And he was going to love the irritation.

Laying her head on his shoulder, Quinn snuggled against him, rooting around until their bodies fit perfectly together.

They were quiet for several moments. Jace listened to the even cadence of her breath. Absorbed the weight and heat of it as it brushed across his naked chest.

And he was grateful. For the moment. For Quinn.

For what Michael had given him. Them.

He'd spent his life looking out for his little brother and didn't begrudge a single sacrifice he'd ever made. Would have made a thousand more if it meant Michael's happiness.

So why was he fighting against accepting the single biggest sacrifice Michael had ever made for him? No, he hadn't willingly stepped aside for them, but Jace knew if he was standing there beside them today, he would have.

If he'd known just how much Jace loved her.

He wasn't even positive when it had happened. Certainly not in the past few days. Long before that, although there was a new underlying burn to the emotion.

Quinn rubbed her cheek against him, purring softly in the back of her throat. With a soft chuckle, she brushed her lips against him. The thrill was there, a jagged bolt of need, but overlaid by a soft peace he hadn't felt in a very long time.

"Do you remember when he…" Quinn's words carried on, reliving some moment they'd all shared together. He could hear her laughter, feel the curve of it in her mouth pressed against his skin.

His own body reacted, adding a chuckle when appropriate even though he couldn't have remembered the exact words she'd spoken if someone held a gun to his head.

Michael was there. Jace could feel him. But instead of holding them apart, as his memory had done for the past two years, he was drawing them together.

Shared memories and experiences.

It was the first time since Michael had died that Jace thought about his brother and smiled.

She'd given him that.

QUINN WASN'T SURE what had changed, but something had. The restless energy that drove Jace had…quieted. It wasn't gone entirely, more like simply banked until he needed it again.

The guilt that had permanently resided deep in those beautiful blue eyes whenever he looked at her had lost some of its power and hold. Hopefully, one day it would fade completely.

They woke tangled together in a comfortable, easy way. Sharing a shower had just solidified the rightness of the moment.

Needing to feel him on her skin even as they tried to move on to mundane things, she'd slipped on one of his long-sleeved plaid shirts. The tails brushed the backs of her thighs and the sleeves were so long she'd had to roll them several times. But the way he'd looked at her when she'd walked into the kitchen had made it worth it. Not to mention that whenever she turned her head she'd get a lungful of his amazing scent.

He'd only thrown on a pair of worn sweatpants so threadbare she could practically see his tanned skin showing through. He looked amazing and part of her wanted to drag him back to bed. It wasn't as if they had much planned for the day, anyway.

But there was a part of her that felt they needed to act like normal adults instead of hormone-laden teenagers. This wasn't just about lust. It was more. Somehow eating the breakfast he made and sharing a cup of coffee made her feel as if this was real and not just something fleeting and grounded in their forced proximity.

It made her think this would go on long after he no longer needed to protect her.

Although that only went so far. Since he'd cooked, Quinn cleaned away the breakfast dishes leaving him to sip on his second cup of coffee while scanning through the news on a tablet.

She was wandering over to pick up her own cup, intending to refresh it, when his arm snaked out, snagging her waist, and she tumbled into his lap. Until that moment she would have said he wasn't paying any attention to her.

Obviously, she was wrong. Jace could definitely multitask.

His gaze didn't drift away from the screen of his tablet. Not even when she struggled—half-heartedly—to get up. The band of his arm just tightened, holding her in place.

Finally shrugging, Quinn leaned across the table and stole his coffee. He growled a playful warning even as

the corners of his mouth tipped up into a barely suppressed smile.

"The price of not letting me up to get my own."

He nuzzled her neck for a moment, trailing his mouth
up to her ear where he rumbled, "Worth it," sending a
shiver tripping across her skin.

The whole thing was very domestic. Quinn could see
herself doing this with him every Saturday and Sunday
for the rest of her life. She wanted it.

So much it scared her. This was so new. Was she setting herself up for heartache by building a future—even
if only in her head—with him so quickly?

He must have sensed the tension in her body, because
he abandoned the tablet, shifting his hold on her until
she was facing him.

"Hey. What's wrong?"

Quinn shook her head. It was too early. She couldn't
tell him she was falling for him. Not yet. Apprehension fluttered in her chest, uncomfortable and chilling.

"Nothing." And because she knew he wouldn't believe that, she pulled out a lie. "Just thinking about my
place."

His arms around her waist tightened. Touching his
forehead to hers, he brought them close. "It's going to
be fine. Like you said, they're just things. They can be
replaced."

Pulling back, he flashed her a smile that was more
than half devil. "Look on the bright side. You get to go
shopping. With someone else's money."

That really did make her think about all the things
she needed to do today. Like contact her insurance company and start the process of filing a claim. No doubt
they'd want the police report....

Quinn frowned. "Could we just go back to bed and pretend it's still the middle of the night?"

Fingers coaxing beneath her chin, Jace brought her face around until he could claim her mouth. It was so easy to sink down into the pull of his kiss. "Absolutely," he murmured against her lips.

Unfortunately, the sound of her phone broke into the heat he was building between them. It was her ringtone for work. They knew she wasn't coming in—probably for the rest of the week. But a couple of her colleagues had called to ask questions about her cases they'd taken over.

Pulling away, Quinn gave him an apologetic smile. "I'm sorry. I have to take that."

He sighed, the look in his eyes close to how a five-year-old would react to losing his favorite toy. But he loosened his hold on her, giving her room to climb off his lap.

Rounding the counter, she pulled her phone from her purse where she'd left it near the door last night. Thinking it would be a routine conversation, she dropped onto the sofa, folding her legs beneath her and tucking the edges of Jace's shirt around her thighs.

"Hey, Daniel. What's up?"

It was obvious from the first words out of his mouth that this wasn't going to be an easy conversation.

"I'm sorry, Quinn. You know I wouldn't be asking you this if there was any other way."

"Ask me what?" Quinn said, sitting up straight and dropping her feet back to the floor. For some reason, her body was taut, already in fight-or-flight mode.

Apparently sensing the change in her demeanor, or maybe hearing it in her voice, Jace appeared in the doorway between the kitchen and living room. Reaching up, he grasped the lintel and stretched his body. She was beginning to realize the move was a nervous habit.

Although she liked the way it highlighted his muscles, especially when he wasn't wearing a shirt.

"It's Ana Martinez."

Oh, hell. Ana was nineteen, technically an adult, but she'd been a runaway when Quinn had first started working with her two years ago. She'd convinced Ana to contact her mother and try to mend whatever was broken.

Her mother, heartsick when her daughter had disappeared, had been so happy to hear from Ana. Things had been going well, until her mother started seeing a new man. Quinn knew something was wrong, but Ana wouldn't open up and tell her. Until she did, there was little she could do aside from be there when Ana needed a friend.

"What about Ana," she asked cautiously.

"She was waiting out back when Michelle got here this morning."

"Okay."

"She's been beaten. And from the looks of some of the bruises, more than once."

Oh, God. Quinn's stomach clenched. It was a good thing she was here and not there. This kind of reaction wouldn't help Ana, but she wasn't sure she could have controlled it. Wrapping an arm around her middle, she tried to keep the helpless rage from spilling out.

"Who's taking her case?"

"That's just it. She won't talk to anyone else. I think…" Daniel's voice trailed off.

He cleared his throat. It wasn't often her boss was

overwhelmed by emotion. He'd been at this longer than she had, and while he was one of the best men she'd ever met, there was a part of him that had been hardened to some of the struggles they saw over and over again. This wasn't going to be good.

"I think she was raped, Quinn. But she won't answer our questions. We need to find out for sure and get a rape kit."

Jesus, what was wrong with humanity?

Quinn was up off the sofa and headed for the bedroom before she was even conscious she'd made a decision to move. "I'll be there in fifteen. Just tell her I'm on my way."

"Thanks, Quinn," Daniel said, his voice full of relief.

Tossing her phone onto the bed, she was scrambling through her bag when a hard voice sounded behind her.

"You're not going."

Throwing the briefest glance over her shoulder, Quinn said, "I am."

This wasn't up for debate. But apparently, Jace was hell-bent on having one anyway.

Grasping her shoulders, he pulled her away from her bag, turning her to face him. "It's too dangerous, Quinn. You can't go to the office. Warren's probably watching it."

"I don't care. I have to go. There's a girl I've been working with for two years, Jace. She came in beaten and bloody. Daniel thinks she's been raped."

She watched the skin around his mouth tighten. Fire flashed in his eyes. And she loved him for it. Not even knowing Ana, he was pissed on her behalf. But even as the instinct to protect flared inside him, she could see his resolve hardening.

"I'm sorry for her, Quinn. But someone else can help her. It doesn't have to be you. Not right now."

"She won't talk to anyone else, Jace. Don't you think Daniel thought of that before calling me? Half an hour, maybe a little more. Just enough to calm her down and find out what happened. After that we can leave."

She stepped to him, bridging the space between them. Wrapping her arms around his waist, she tipped her face up to his, eyes pleading.

"You'll be with me. I'll be fine because I know you won't let anything bad happen to me. Besides, it's the middle of the day. He's been careful so far and I can't see him changing that MO now. He won't make a move that's so visible." Rubbing her hands down his arms in a soothing gesture, she pressed her lips to his. "It'll be fine. I promise."

Jace's mouth stayed stony beneath hers for several seconds before finally softening. It was the moment she knew she had him. Although, that didn't mean he was happy about it.

Spinning away, he jerked his hands through his hair, pausing to tug at the ends near his neck. A string of curses accompanied the gesture.

"Fine," he growled, pinning her with his dangerous, blue gaze. She had no doubt it was the same expression he used on cocky soldiers who thought they knew better than their seasoned brothers. "But only until she's settled. Promise me we'll get in and out quickly."

"Absolutely."

13

HE DIDN'T LIKE IT. But then, he'd made that more than obvious to Quinn. And again on the phone to Daniel.

Although there was a part of him that admired Quinn's selfless heart and her need to help anyone in trouble, it really bothered him that her generosity could come with a price. One they'd both pay.

Because if something happened to her, he didn't know what he'd do.

Parking as close to the door as he could manage, Jace rushed Quinn into the building, more comfortable once she was safely inside.

Although not even that could temper the sense of foreboding lodged at the base of his neck. After years in hostile locations, he had a highly honed sense of danger. Sometimes all you had to warn you were your instincts that said something was off. And those instincts were screaming at him, even though not a single thing was out of place.

Before following Quinn inside, he scanned their lot, as well as the ones on either side and across the road.

He watched the windows in the other office buildings. Nothing.

Maybe he was just on edge because it was Quinn.

Heading inside, he went in search of her.

Knocking softly on the closed door one of the other women in the office directed him to, he stopped just inside the doorway when Quinn's soft voice told him to come in.

The girl she was sitting next to had obviously been beaten. She had bruises covering her face, one bleeding into another. The corner of her lip was busted and there were shallow cuts, as if from someone's dirty finger-nails, down both of her arms. Not deep enough to need attention, but red enough that they'd obviously bled.

She barely flicked him a glance, keeping her gaze trained on Quinn's face.

It was probably a good thing Jace didn't know who'd done this to the girl, because if he had he'd have been first in line to kick some ass. And he knew several men—soldiers and fighters both—who'd be more than willing to stand beside him to make sure the lesson took.

Murmuring that he'd be outside, Jace left the two women alone. He propped his back against the wall opposite the door, crossed his arms over his chest and waited, no longer protecting one but two.

Through the wide window in the door, he could see them both. He watched Quinn comfort the girl as tears streamed unchecked down Ana's cheeks.

He didn't say a word when Quinn's half hour came and went. He did insist Daniel send out for some food, though, when they hit four hours and it was well past lunchtime. Quinn would never forgive him if he insisted she leave. And, after seeing Ana, he understood why. The girl was a tiny slip of a thing.

The warning jangling across his skin didn't dissipate, but he knew that inside the building Quinn was as safe as he could make her for the moment.

He was afraid the fallout would come later. Maybe it was time to think about leaving his place. No doubt Warren had discovered who Jace was by now—and his address. When they left here he'd get a hotel for tonight and they could talk about other options tomorrow.

Through the day, he'd heard the low murmur of Quinn's voice, punctuated occasionally with Ana's soft sobs. Two officers walked into the room—a woman and a man. Quinn greeted them by name, which helped to settle Jace's nerves a little.

They spent the next hour with Quinn holding Ana's hand as the officers asked questions, made notes and began the process of apprehending Ana's assailant.

When they finally left, Ana, completely drained, lay down on the soft bed on the far side of the room and fell asleep.

Quinn's shoulders slumped and her head dropped as if she didn't have the energy to hold it up anymore.

Opening the door, Jace quietly crossed to her and smoothed his hands over her shoulders. He dug his thumbs into the top of her spine, rubbing rhythmically.

She let out a rich hum, the vibration traveling up from her body and into his. "That feels amazing," she whispered.

He hated seeing her like this—physically exhausted and mentally drained. He knew why she did it. Understood that the need to help people was so deeply ingrained she couldn't separate it from any other part of herself.

But seeing the toll it had on her, he wanted to protect her from everything that could potentially hurt her, even if the harm was self-inflicted. But that wasn't always possible.

"We need to leave," he finally said.

"I know. But I want to wait a little while longer." Tipping her head back, Quinn buried the crown of her head in his stomach, her gaze finding his. "In case she has nightmares."

She didn't have to explain. The memory of her own nightmare rose up between them, full of the ghosts she'd have to battle over and over again because they never quite went away.

Jace's chest tightened—for her and for the girl. He hated that either of them had to live with such sad, frightening memories.

But while he was worrying about what caused their nightmares, apparently Quinn was concentrating on how her last nightmare, that single moment of vulnerability, had finally brought them together.

Suddenly the space between them was heavy with a familiar heat. He could *feel* her awareness and need like a caress across his overly sensitized skin.

But now wasn't the time or place.

Pulling back, he said, "All right. But we can't stay long. I want to leave before it gets dark."

She nodded, reaching up to grasp his hand where it curved across her shoulder. Picking it up, she brought it to her mouth, pressing a kiss to the center of his palm.

"Have I told you what an amazing man you are?"

Jace shook his head. "You're the amazing one." They both gazed at Ana curled up on the bed not far away.

"I should have stopped it," she whispered, anguish filling the words. "I knew something was wrong, but

I didn't think it was this bad. I thought they didn't get along, you know—new man who wasn't her father stepping in to take some control. That's not easy in the best of circumstances, but add a teenager struggling to find her independence to the mix and it almost always leads to clashing wills."

Jace felt moisture hit his fingers and roll between them.

Crouching beside her, he urged her to look at him. Her deep, dark eyes were luminous with tears, full of regret and the kind of guilt he recognized because he'd been carrying it around for too long.

"I had no idea the guy was raping her. Last night wasn't the first time. But it was the first time he let his friends have a turn."

"Sonofabitch," Jace breathed. His fists clenched, shaking with the driving need to hurt something—someone.

"Yep. Her mom had to go out of town for a few days. Sick aunt. Ana was planning on staying with a friend. She went home to pick up a few things while she thought the house was empty. It wasn't. He was there waiting for her."

"It's not your fault."

"I know," she sighed, but Jace didn't believe her. She was paying lip service to what she was supposed to say. He recognized that, too, having done enough of it himself since Michael died.

"It's not your fault."

"Yeah."

Jace's grasp on her chin tightened. Her gaze flew to his, wide and haunted. "You didn't hurt her, Quinn. You put your own life in danger to be here. You're the one who saved her. You were there when she needed someone. And you'll be there every step of the way as she deals with the aftermath. You can't always stop bad things from happening. The only thing you can do is be there to help when they do."

She swallowed, her eyes swimming with tears. He could see the swell of the emotion she'd been holding back all day because Ana had needed her to be strong. But Quinn didn't need to be strong anymore. He was here now, able to take some of the weight off her shoulders, even if he'd never be able to convince her to give it up altogether.

Not that he'd want to. Because asking her to do that would be asking her to change who she was.

And he loved who she was.

Picking her up, he settled back into her chair. Her body curled into a tight ball, knees next to his ribs, hands clenched in his shirt and face buried in his neck.

She cried quietly. Even in the midst of her own emotional storm, she didn't want to disturb Ana's few moments of relief. Her hot tears soaked his shirt, and his hands rubbed up and down her trembling back.

All he wanted to do was make it better, but there was no way he could fix this.

The realization left him restless and only increased the apprehension he'd been fighting for the past several hours.

IT WAS DARK by the time they left. Quinn was exhausted—emotionally and physically. But Ana was going to be okay, because Quinn wouldn't let anything else happen.

They were in the process of finding her a safe place

to stay, connecting her with a support group and getting her long-term help. Quinn had sat at her side when she'd made the call to her mother—who was now on her way home to be with Ana.

It was a relief to realize Ana would have that support, as well. Her mother had honestly had no idea what had been going on.

Keeping Quinn in the shelter of his body, Jace ushered them through the lot. He waited until she was settled before closing the passenger-side door and rounding the hood.

Jeez, she was tired. Physically and emotionally drained. And the thought of going home, putting on comfy clothes and curling up beside Jace was the best thing she'd ever heard of.

Maybe she dozed off or just zoned out. She'd never be quite certain. But one moment she was sitting in the quiet cab of the truck, the next the door was squealing open and a gun was pointed straight at her forehead.

"Move over." Warren's wild gaze bored into her across the barrel.

That look of madness, more than anything, had her stomach clenching with dread.

Without taking her gaze from him, she began to inch sideways across the bench seat.

"Don't even think about it," he growled, his eyes flicking quickly away and out the windshield.

Quinn followed his gaze straight to Jace, who stood immobilized on the other side of the hood.

His hand hovered beside his hip. Quinn knew his gun was tucked there, but apparently Warren did, as well.

"Before you can pull it she'll be dead."

A rough hand tightened around her upper arm, anchoring her in place. She felt the imprint of each finger on her skin. But that didn't matter.

Not when she could see the panic, guilt and crystal-clear agony in Jace's eyes.

He was going to blame himself for this, too.

Regret twisted deep inside her. Not for herself, but for him.

"He's going to walk over here and hand you the keys. If either of you try anything I'm going to put a bullet in your side. It won't be enough to kill you, at least, not right away. That way you'll be conscious when I put another one through his skull."

A fine tremor invaded her hands. Quinn balled them tight to hide the reaction.

"Do you understand?"

She gave him a short, jerky nod and listened as he yelled basically the same warning out to Jace.

His clear blue eyes flared with frustration and impotent rage. She watched it flood his face, red just beneath tanned skin. His jaw clamped tight.

She could tell he was trying to find an angle that would get her out of this. But even she realized there wasn't one. At least not one that didn't end up with one of them bleeding from a bullet hole.

But she knew Jace and if there was a way to save her by sacrificing himself he'd do it.

Snagging his gaze through the windshield, she slowly shook her head. This wasn't the time for action. And even if he didn't want to admit it, he realized the truth in what she was telling him.

With deliberate steps, Jace walked up to the edge of the open driver's-side window. When he held the keys out in front of him, she let her fingers brush across his. The heat that was always there when they touched blasted up her arm.

It was comforting. Just the surge of energy she needed to keep her calm.

"I'll get you out of this," he murmured. The promise behind his words steadied her.

Jace would do everything in his power to help her.

"As long as she does what I want, she'll be fine. Now, back away. I want you inside the building before we leave."

Jace hesitated.

"The longer we sit here, Mr. Hyland, the itchier my trigger finger gets. I might accidentally shoot her knee or shoulder."

With a growl of pure frustration, Jace began moving away. Quinn watched him, at first through the windshield and then through the rearview mirror.

Beside her, Warren turned in his seat but managed to keep the gun trained straight on her chest. "Ms. Keller, start the engine. And take me to my wife."

Easing out of the parking space, she headed to the edge of the lot and the street. She had a decision to make—which direction.

She had several things going for her. There was no doubt in her head that Jace was already on the phone with the police, reporting his stolen truck and her kidnapping. It wouldn't be long before the cavalry arrived.

Unfortunately, she didn't think they were going to be much help. In fact, they might do more damage.

"I won't hesitate to shoot you, Ms. Keller, so let's be smart."

Quinn turned her head to look at the man currently

holding her at gunpoint. She hadn't seen him in several days. And it was clear that time hadn't been kind.

The man who'd walked into their office looking for his wife had been expensively dressed, confident in his power and certain he could talk his way into what he wanted.

The man sitting beside her was disheveled, his perfectly cut hair now bright with the sheen of grease. His clothes were wrinkled and frankly, he needed a shower.

But all of that was nothing to Quinn.

What sent a spike of pure fear through her was the maniacal gleam in his eyes.

He was unhinged. Something had clearly snapped.

If the cops screamed in, surrounding this truck, she didn't think she would make it out. The crazed man beside her would just shoot them both.

And she really didn't want to die this way.

One thing was certain, though—she'd let him shoot her before leading him to Caroline. But maybe those weren't her only two options.

On her side was the fact that Warren had no idea where the safe house was located so she could string him along for a few minutes at least. A few minutes for him to make a mistake. And for her to think.

Although maybe that wasn't the best thing. Thoughts of her family flashed through her mind. She'd always wanted a better relationship with her sister, but had never really pushed for it. If she had it to do over again, she'd try harder.

Her parents. Losing them the way she had…it was hard. Especially being the only one to survive the accident. Quinn's hands began to tremble on the wheel so she gripped it harder.

They'd loved her so much. Been the kind of people who would have given their last dollar if someone really needed it. She'd grown up knowing she wanted to be like them, grateful for the example they'd set for her.

Jace. Her vision blurred. Quinn tried to force the reaction away—she needed to be able to see.

Honestly, he was the one regret she had. Not that they'd found each other, but that they'd both fought it for two years. Needlessly denied themselves that time together.

This was going to kill him. He took so much responsibility onto his shoulders—responsibility that wasn't necessarily his to carry. She knew him, and no matter what anyone else told him, he'd see this as a failure. His failure.

He was supposed to protect her and he hadn't been successful. At least in his own eyes.

He hadn't learned the lesson life had forced on her at such a young age. There is no such thing as control. There were forces out there, bigger than any one person, throwing people together and tearing them apart.

Random things happened and there was nothing you could do. No one could plan for every possibility.

Quinn closed her eyes. A major intersection came into view ahead of them. Out of the corner of her eye she could see Warren's leg bouncing up and down as if he couldn't keep it still. He kept watching her, the laser focus of his stare sending a chill racing down her spine.

She didn't have much time.

There was a concrete retaining wall coming up on the right. It was low, but high enough.

The plan didn't so much form as pop into her head

fully realized. Maybe because she'd been thinking about her parents' accident.

A hundred yards ahead, she saw the first brush of the gray brick. Her hands gripped tighter around the wheel, straining to hold course.

Panic seized her. Her nightmare burst full force, past overlaying present in a sickening memory that left her panting. Sweat beaded along her hairline. Her brain screamed at her not to do it, but calm resolve pushed the warning away.

The sound of metal crunching. Her mother's scream—her own name—cut off before it was finished. That damn horn that just wouldn't stop. Darkness. Loneliness. Fear.

Those memories had haunted her for years. But today, instead of leaving her weak, they made her strong.

When the edge of the wall was only ten yards away, Quinn checked to make sure there was no one else around her who could get caught up in the disaster she was about to unleash.

Five yards away. Quinn took a deep breath, held it, and jerked the wheel hard, slamming the passenger side into cold concrete.

Warren yelled. Quinn screwed her eyes shut, waiting for the bullet she'd expected to go flying, but it never came. That same screech of metal filled her head. The truck lurched and then somehow they were flying.

That was not part of the plan.

The truck twisted in the air, rolling once before landing on dirt and grass. It skidded, tearing up the ground beneath them. Quinn's head smacked into something hard. Her chest slammed against the steering wheel before her belt and airbag propelled her backward into the seat.

Her body felt as though it was being battered from the inside, organs, bone and muscle knocking against sinew, tendons and skin. Straining. Fighting against whatever held them in place. She almost wished they'd just snap and save her the unbelievable tension and pain.

And then it was over. The sickening motion stopped and by some miracle she was still breathing.

Blinking, it took several seconds for all the sounds to filter in. People yelling. The engine still racing. Her vision was blurry, everything overlaid with a watery film that seemed to come straight from the pounding pain in her head.

Her thoughts were erratic, bouncing all over the place and settling nowhere. Her movements even worse. But she was obviously upside down, held in place by the belt across her hips and shoulder. The pressure was almost unbearable, constricting her lungs and making her panic.

With a shaky hand she reached for the release. Her fingers slipped across the button, somehow finding the strength to push hard.

But she couldn't make it let her go.

Colors sparkled across her vision—blue, pink, yellow and green. The world swam in and out of focus. Her head hurt like hell. And she couldn't get a full breath, making it all worse.

Everything was sluggish, her brain, her body, her thoughts. She dragged her gaze through the car, registering the bent and broken console, until she lighted on Warren.

His body was twisted and broken. Just like her parents' had been. One arm hung limply above his head, bent at an angle that wasn't natural. Blood soaked into the front of his wrinkled white dress shirt. More leaked slowly down his face, drip, drip, dripping onto the roof they were both suspended over.

Oh, God, what had she done?

Regret and guilt twisted inside her. Until, with a gasp, his eyes popped open

He stared straight into her, completely cracked. All that was left was the crazed madman she'd gotten glimpses of over the past few days.

Warren began to flail, his useless feet kicking out against the crumpled dash pinning them both in. The arm over his head swung back and forth, freely, as if all the ligaments and muscles had been stripped away and the only thing keeping it attached was his skin.

Bile rose in the back of Quinn's throat.

He screamed, unintelligible words tumbling from his open mouth. Thank God he no longer held the gun, because in that moment she knew he would have shot her over and over again if he'd had the option.

She needed to get out of here. Redoubling her efforts, Quinn finally managed to unbuckle her belt. But without the nylon straps taking her weight, gravity returned, crashing her to the ceiling of the truck with a force that left her squealing in pain.

Her vision swam again, bursting to black before colors shot through again, mirroring the waves of pain assaulting her body.

Reality and memory melded, Warren morphing from himself into her parents and then back.

She was going to black out. No, she couldn't. Not yet. Pulling up an image of Jace, looking at her as if he could see straight to her soul—and liked what he saw—she took it, used it. Forced herself to push back the wave of blackness that threatened to consume her and find a well of strength deep down inside.

Reaching for the door handle, she lifted and shoved. But nothing happened.

The scent of gasoline filled her head making her even dizzier. And then smoke. Something was on fire. And she was trapped.

No, she wasn't going to die. She couldn't do that to Jace.

With a cry, Quinn marshaled the last of her strength to shove at the mangled door trapping her inside, but it wouldn't budge.

And with nothing left, she couldn't hold back the darkness anymore.

14

OH, GOD. JACE stood behind the glass door, fear and frenzy turning his stomach. He'd lived through a war zone. Watched friends die. Watched his brother die.

This was so much worse. Standing there, knowing Quinn was in trouble and being unable to do anything to protect her.

He yelled for Daniel, dialing 911 at the same time.

The operator did her job, but all her questions frustrated him. He told the woman Quinn had been kidnapped at gunpoint and taken in his stolen truck. He reeled off the license plate and description.

The police were on her trail thirty seconds after she and Warren were out of the parking lot. But it wasn't enough.

Daniel came running, and Jace didn't even have to demand keys to a car before they were being pushed into his palm.

He was going to kill Warren. With his bare hands.

He was no more than a couple of minutes behind them when he peeled out of the lot.

Even as he headed in the direction Quinn had turned,

he tried to reason his way into a calm he did not feel. Warren wanted his wife and Quinn knew where Caroline was. He wouldn't hurt her until they had Caroline.

Unfortunately, he didn't think Quinn would actually take him anywhere near the other woman. Which was good and bad—good for Caroline, but bad for Quinn.

Eventually, Warren would figure out she was stringing him along. And then... Jace's stomach clenched tight with dread.

He heard the accident. The sickening grind of metal and several loud bangs.

As his car screamed around the corner, he saw the truck upside down in the grass beside the overpass, wheels spinning lazily, and felt his gorge rise.

Even in the few moments before he arrived the crash was already attracting a crowd.

His borrowed car tore through grass as he slid to a stop several feet away. The driver's-side door swung drunkenly behind him as he raced across the remaining space.

Several people were scrambling around the crumpled truck. Others held cells to their ears, probably calling in the accident. Jace didn't bother with that. His one and only concern was getting to Quinn.

The truck was totaled, crunched in the front and sides, and settled on the cab. The astringent scent of gas filled the air and a couple of people who'd obviously realized the danger were trying to push back the gathering spectators.

Two men were trying to pry off the passenger side door. Others were doing the same at the driver's side. Jace skidded to his knees, trying to look inside and find her.

Adrenaline and fear pumped straight into his veins at the sight that greeted him. There was blood everywhere, but luckily he thought most of it was coming from Warren and not Quinn.

Somehow she'd managed to get out of her belt, but was crumpled into a heap on the inverted ceiling of his truck. Her hand lay on the door handle, as if she'd been trying to escape, but her eyes were closed and her body still.

At least she'd been conscious at some point after the accident.

But there was no way they were getting the driver's door open. It was too banged up. Quickly assessing the situation, Jace grabbed a large rock and headed to the back windshield. Using all his strength, he pounded on it several times before it finally started to give, a spiderweb forming across the surface.

The sound of crackling glass had never been so sweet.

In the distance, he could hear sirens wailing, but they weren't going to get here in time. Black smoke drifted into the gathering dusk, burning his lungs with apprehension. Something was on fire and when it reached the gas tank...

Ignoring the shards of glass cutting into his palms, arms and legs, Jace crawled through the opening he'd made and managed to grasp Quinn around the waist and tug.

Tucking her against his body, Jace backed out, careful to keep her from being cut by the shards everywhere. It took too long. His heart thumped erratically the entire time—he was certain the fire was going to reach the gas tank at any moment.

But at least if they went, they were going together.

People were yelling at him. Someone else was impatiently waiting to climb in through the hole he'd made, but Jace screamed at him to back away so he could get Quinn safe.

Once they were free, Jace didn't stop until they were thirty yards away, then he finally collapsed to the ground with her.

The way her body flopped, limp and lifeless, scared the shit out of him. Cradling her in his lap, Jace ran his hands over her, frantically searching for a pulse and breath.

A little of his panic ebbed when he found both. What bothered him was the gigantic knot coming up on the side of her head.

Several emergency teams sped onto the scene, sirens blaring. Police and firefighters pushed everyone back from the truck. Warren was still trapped inside, but it was too dangerous to attempt a rescue until that fire was out.

The firemen began unwinding the hose that would extinguish the flames now curling up through the engine of the car.

Jace didn't think they were going to make it in time. He could see orange, red and yellow fingers of flame licking several feet into the sky.

And then the whole world exploded. Or, at least, it felt that way. Jace had been close to several bomb detonations. But this was different. The reverberation of it rattled his chest. Instinctively, he curled around Quinn's body shielding her from the heat and raining debris.

Several people screamed. A few were tossed backward by the force of the blast. The firefighters began blanketing the roaring pile of metal with foam.

Warren hadn't gotten out. Jace couldn't find a single piece of his soul upset about that fact.

Smoothing Quinn's disheveled hair back from her face, Jace bent close and called to her. "Quinn, sweetheart, wake up. Please. Let me see those gorgeous eyes."

Her lids fluttered and then opened slowly, as if weighted down by the force of her need to sleep. Her eyes were glazed with shock and pain, her pupils tight little pinpoints, but she was still looking at him. Cognizant. Her tongue slipped out, brushing across her plump lips. "Sorry about your truck," she croaked.

Jace groaned, the sound a combination of relief and mangled laughter. "Don't worry about it."

But the relief was short-lived, quickly replaced by the toxic sludge of fear and frustration and panic he'd been holding back. "What the hell were you thinking?"

Her lips twisted. "I was trying to smash his side of the car. Didn't plan on the roll."

Yeah, because knowing that made it all better. Jace's arms tightened around her. She winced, her eyes closing. For a moment he thought she'd passed out again, but she kept talking.

"I couldn't let him get to Caroline."

Sweet heaven above. Jace wasn't sure what he wanted to do most, shake some sense into her or kiss the hell out of that smart, sassy, beautiful mouth.

She took the decision away from him, opening her eyes, she stared straight up into his face. A soft smile touched her lips right before she lifted her head, sealing her lips to his. The zing through his blood was immediate. His heart rate, only just now returning to normal, kicked high again.

Breaking the kiss, Jace pulled away and felt the words he'd been keeping bottled up finally spill out.

"God, Quinn. I don't know what I would have done if something had happened to you. You're my world. My everything. I love you so much."

Her chin trembled and her eyes shimmered with tears. "Say that again."

Jace sucked in a hard breath, realization slamming into him. The words had just tumbled out the first time. This time he made a conscious decision to say them.

Tangling his fingers in her hair, he carefully shifted them both until they were as close as possible. "I love you, Quinn. I've loved you for a long time. I'm through feeling guilty for wanting you, for needing you in my life."

Her hands found his face, bracketing both sides. "I love you, too, Jace. I'm not sure when it happened, maybe a long time ago. But I need you, more than I think you'll ever know. I can't imagine a single day of my life without you."

Jace leaned in to take her mouth again, needing the feel and taste of her. The reassurance that she really was alive and with him.

A voice cleared beside them, breaking into the moment. "Uh, ma'am, someone said you were inside the car? We need to get you checked out."

Epilogue

JACE COULDN'T KEEP STILL. He wasn't used to being this nervous about anything. Bouncing on the balls of his feet, he shoved his hands deep into the pockets of his pants to try and hide the slight tremble he couldn't seem to will away.

He didn't want anyone to think he was having second thoughts. Not at all. He was just anxious to get this over with so he could call Quinn his wife.

The doors at the opposite end of the room opened. She stood, framed in the entryway, and for a moment he forgot how to breathe.

She was beautiful. Luminous and gorgeous and in about fifteen minutes his forever. At least according to the state of Georgia and a piece of paper. She'd been his in his head long before today.

Her gaze was trained solely on him, bright and clear. He could see love shining out of her light brown eyes and knew the same thing filled his own. Could feel it filling him up and spilling over.

The room could have been completely empty, the way they focused on each other, although it wasn't.

However, there were only a handful of people present. They'd both agreed that a small ceremony was the way to go. Their immediate family and a group of close friends. His parents, her sister. Daniel and several of Quinn's friends from work. A few of his Ranger buddies, the ones who'd been able to get here on short notice. Caroline, whom Quinn had become very close to in the past few months.

Warren had died in the accident, leaving Caroline finally free—not to mention very wealthy. She'd immediately started working with Quinn and Daniel to donate a healthy chunk of her wealth to their program.

Quinn had struggled for the first few weeks, feeling responsible for Warren's death. It had opened up several discussions between them, and even as she'd worked through her own issues, she'd somehow managed to help him with his lingering guilt over Michael's death.

He would never be okay with losing his brother, but he was finally willing to admit nothing he could have done would have changed the outcome.

They both agreed Michael would be thrilled that they were happy and had found their way to each other.

Quinn stopped beside Jace, reaching for his hand. He turned his back on the people around them, focusing solely on the woman in front of him.

For two years he'd tried to convince himself she wasn't for him, when there was nothing further from the truth. Quinn Keller was perfect for him—and he was perfect for her.

They complemented each other, pushing each other out of their comfort zones. She reminded him there was gentleness and goodness in the world. And he calmed her, centered her, convinced her that sometimes you had to put yourself first so you had something left to give when it was needed.

The minister read the words of the ceremony. They both repeated their vows and slipped gleaming bands on each other's fingers.

Wrapping his arms around her, Jace pulled his wife close and kissed her, hard. A smattering of applause surrounded them as their family crowded in.

And Jace swore he could hear the ghost of a laugh that sent a shiver down his spine and had the hairs on the back of his neck standing on end. He watched goose bumps spread across Quinn's skin. Her eyes snagged his, understanding drifting between them.

Lifting up on her toes, Quinn kissed him again, whispering against his lips, "I'm so grateful that Warren brought us together. I'd go through it all again if it meant I got to end up here, with you as my husband."

Jace wasn't entirely certain he agreed with her. Pulling her limp body out of that wreckage was a nightmare he never wanted to relive. But she did have a point. Every step they'd made together had led them to this moment.

And every step afterward they'd share together.

* * * * *

#803 RIDING HARD
Sons of Chance • by Vicki Lewis Thompson

Large animal vet Drake Brewster might have just come to her rescue, but Tracy Gibbons knows the seemingly perfect Southern gentleman is still a no-good heartbreaker. So why can't she keep her hands off him?

#804 DOUBLE EXPOSURE
From Every Angle • by Erin McCarthy

Posing with hundreds of people wearing only body paint? Career journalist Emma Gideon agrees, just to get her story. And when she ends up in bed with rival journalist Kyle Hadley, more than just their skin is exposed....

#805 WICKED SEXY
Uniformly Hot! • by Anne Marsh

Search-and-rescue swimmer Daeg Ross is used to jumping into treacherous waters. But his feelings for relationship-shy Dani Andrews are a whole new type of risk. Together, will they sink...or swim?

#806 TAKEN BY STORM
by Heather MacAllister

When a blizzard leaves her stranded, Zoey is desperate for a way to get across the country. Luckily, a sexy and charming Texan offers her just the ride she needs....

REQUEST YOUR FREE BOOKS!
2 FREE NOVELS PLUS 2 FREE GIFTS!

HARLEQUIN®

Blaze®

red-hot reads!

YES! Please send me 2 FREE Harlequin® Blaze™ novels and my 2 FREE gifts (gifts are worth about $10). After receiving them, if I don't wish to receive any more books, I can return the shipping statement marked "cancel." If I don't cancel, I will receive 4 brand-new novels every month and be billed just $4.74 per book in the U.S. or $4.96 per book in Canada. That's a savings of at least 14% off the cover price. It's quite a bargain. Shipping and handling is just 50¢ per book in the U.S. and 75¢ per book in Canada. I understand that accepting the 2 free books and gifts places me under no obligation to buy anything. I can always return a shipment and cancel at any time. Even if I never buy another book, the two free books and gifts are mine to keep forever.

150/350 HDN F4WC

Name	(PLEASE PRINT)

Address		Apt. #

City	State/Prov.	Zip/Postal Code

Signature (if under 18, a parent or guardian must sign)

Mail to the **Harlequin® Reader Service:**
IN U.S.A.: P.O. Box 1867, Buffalo, NY 14240-1867
IN CANADA: P.O. Box 609, Fort Erie, Ontario L2A 5X3

Want to try two free books from another line?
Call 1-800-873-8635 or visit www.ReaderService.com.

* Terms and prices subject to change without notice. Prices do not include applicable taxes. Sales tax applicable in N.Y. Canadian residents will be charged applicable taxes. Offer not valid in Quebec. This offer is limited to one order per household. Not valid for current subscribers to Harlequin Blaze books. All orders subject to credit approval. Credit or debit balances in a customer's account(s) may be offset by any other outstanding balance owed by or to the customer. Please allow 4 to 6 weeks for delivery. Offer available while quantities last.

Your Privacy—The Harlequin® Reader Service is committed to protecting your privacy. Our Privacy Policy is available online at www.ReaderService.com or upon request from the Harlequin Reader Service.

We make a portion of our mailing list available to reputable third parties that offer products we believe may interest you. If you prefer that we not exchange your name with third parties, or if you wish to clarify or modify your communication preferences, please visit us at www.ReaderService.com/consumerchoice or write to us at Harlequin Reader Service Preference Service, P.O. Box 9062, Buffalo, NY 14269. Include your complete name and address.

HB13R2

Emma shifted on the seat of Kyle's car, hoping she wasn't
smearing paint onto the upholstery. Why on earth had she
volunteered to do this stupid group photo shoot? With the
coworker she secretly craved, no less? The sooner she got this
paint off and some clothes on, the sooner sanity would reappear.

"Can I take a shower at your place?" Maybe properly clothed
she would be less aware of Kyle and her reaction to him. Because she could not, would not—ever—indulge herself with
Kyle. Dating and sex made people emotional and irrational.
It didn't mix with work.

"Of course you can." Kyle pulled out of the parking lot for
the short trip to his place.

She caught sight of herself in the visor mirror. She looked
worse than she'd thought. There was no way Kyle would ever

come near her like this. Her hair was shot out in all directions, and her skin was emerald-green, with the whites of her eyes and her teeth gleaming in contrast. The napkins she'd used to cover herself tufted up from her chest. "I look like a frog eating barbecue!"

Kyle started laughing so hard he ended up coughing.

"It's not funny!" she protested.

Before they could debate that, he turned in to his building. Still chuckling, he ushered her toward the stairs. "What a day." He tossed his keys onto the table inside the entry of his apartment. "Bathroom's this way. Come on."

Emma followed, her eyes inevitably drawn to his tight butt. He was muscular in an athletic, natural way. Her fingers itched to squeeze all that muscle.

"I'm really good at keeping secrets, you know." Kyle turned, his eyes dark and unreadable.

She was suddenly aware of the sexual tension between them. They were mostly naked, standing inches apart. His mouth was so close....

"If anything happens here today, you can be sure it will never be mentioned at the office."

"What could happen?" She knew what he meant, but she needed to hear confirmation that he was equally attracted to her.

"This." Kyle closed the gap between them.

Emma didn't hesitate, but let her eyes shut as his mouth covered hers in a deep, tantalizing kiss.

Pick up DOUBLE EXPOSURE by Erin McCarthy, available wherever you buy Harlequin® Blaze® books.

Saddle up for a wild ride!

Large-animal vet Drake Brewster might have just come to her rescue, but Tracy Gibbons knows the seemingly perfect Southern gentleman is still a no-good heartbreaker. So why can't she keep her hands off him?

Don't miss the latest in the
Sons of Chance trilogy

Riding Hard

from *New York Times* bestselling author

Vicki Lewis Thompson

Available July 2014, wherever you buy Harlequin Blaze books.

Red-Hot Reads
www.Harlequin.com